Don't Think. Just Breathe.

By Sarah Delany

Dedication

In honour of my Daddio,

John (JD) Delany

Who had the biggest presence in any room and
who left the biggest hole in my heart.

Until we meet again. I hope this makes you proud.

Loving you always,

Your darling daughter.

Contents

Don't Think. Just Breathe.

Tate

Could this party get any more boring? I'd been leaning against this wall for the last thirty minutes watching everyone in the crowded room. I'm surprised I haven't left an imprint of myself on the wall. I have had several people stare at me but ultimately they are all strangers to me other than my cousin JP and his best friend Rafe who dragged me out tonight. Being new in town they thought I needed to mingle. I wanted to stay home and try to get some sleep for once. I'm always so tired but can never sleep. My thoughts keep me awake. Don't think. Don't think. Don't think.

So here I am, surrounded by drunken teenagers but feeling utterly alone. JP and Rafe have ditched me and are nowhere to be seen. There are so many people crammed into this room and not a single one has approached me or tried to make conversation. I guess that's what I get for being the new guy; invisible and easily looked over. It will be a different story once we start school next week. And that's when I spot her; the girl from the other night. This time she's dressed in a simple white strapless dress flowing down past her knees. The skylight above her casting a spotlight on her, illuminating her, giving her the appearance of an angel minus the wings. I wonder if she remembers me? I watch her. She's magnetising and I can't resist the pull. My eyes refuse to leave her. She's so alive and carefree. So different from the girl I came across by chance. She laughs then but it doesn't reach her eyes.

No one else notices. It's all an act. To me she's scared and ready to bolt from her cage at a moment's notice. However, to the ignorant drunken people surrounding her, she is the life of the party.

Her friend spins her around, her dress lifting and twirling with her body. They're having a right old time laughing and spilling their drinks, throwing caution to the wind. She peers around like she can sense someone watching her. She catches my eye and we stare at each other but while my gaze is filled with curiosity, hers is blank. There's no recognition on her face. I don't understand. Does she not remember me? Does she not remember the other night?

JP walks past at that moment and I grab his shoulder.

"Hey, who's the girl?" He follows my gaze and laughs at me when he realises who I'm talking about.

"She's out of your league. Don't waste your breath," he warns.

"But what's her name?" I plead.

"Tamsyn Winter. She's as cold as ice just like her name suggests. Don't go near her unless you're willing to risk frostbite." Tamsyn, aye. Now I have a name to match the face. His description of her is wrong though and so far off the girl I met the other night.

A few nights ago

I can't sleep again so I've ventured out for a run to try and wear myself out. I hope if I push my body to exhaustion, I might finally be able to catch some zzzzs. I run past the dock which has seen better days and catch a glimpse of someone sitting there by themselves. An odd sight for this time of night so I move closer to investigate. As I approach, I notice chocolate brown hair lying in curls half way down a bare hunched back, with elbows resting on their knees. It's a girl. She doesn't appear to be much older than me. Her green halter dress tight against her waist flows out to the sides of her. Slowly she turns and that's when I see her. She looks magical like a fairy. The most piercing blue eyes stare at me. On closer inspection I see they are rimmed with red. She's so broken and defeated.

"Hey, you ok there?" I ask.

"I haven't seen you before, you new here?" She slurs her words a bit, which leads me to believe she might be drunk. The empty bottle of vodka at her feet confirms it.

"Yeah I am," I reply.

"What's your name?" she asks.

"Tate," I tell her.

"Tate, do you know how to swim?"

Stunned by her question I stare at her for a minute before answering, "Yes."

"Great, would you jump in and save me if I was drowning?"

"What?" I screech, thrown off guard.

"Drowning. You know? Can't breathe, going to die, drowning? Would you save me?" she questions.

"Yeah sure I would. You aren't thinking of jumping in now, are you?" She throws her head back and laughs. I stare at her in shock, wondering who this girl is. All of a sudden she pulls herself up to stand and elongates her neck to look me in the eye. Pain reflects in her eyes. What has made this girl so broken? Right now, staring at her I'd do anything to save her if she asked me to.

"Promise?" she whispers.

"Promise," I reply.

"Good. I might hold you to that promise." Like a bullet she is off, sprinting away into the night, her dress and hair whipping behind her. Her bare feet carrying her into the night, leaving me standing there alone, stunned and speechless.

Observing her now, I don't see the broken girl from the dock. The broken girl has been replaced and is hidden behind this act of a bubbly, happy girl who's content to drink lolly water and dance carelessly to teeny bopper music. No one can see the difference. No one can see her struggles. I wonder what she is like. Oh, how I want to know everything about this girl. All I want to do is help her. How can I get her to reveal the girl she so clearly hides from the world? Before I can make my way to her, her friend leads her away through the drunken crowd and just as fast as she came, she's gone again. I wonder if she runs track, she's always moving full speed ahead in the opposite direction, away from me.

The rest of the weekend drags. I spend Sunday with JP in couch potato mode. Cocooned on the faded blue bean bags in his lounge, junk food wrappers engulf us as we button bash each other to death on the Xbox. The highlight of my day is beating JP playing Call of Duty. I mock him, calling him by his full name John Paul (which I know he hates) annoying him enough I keep winning. Mindlessly shooting people and giving my cousin shit is a short reprieve from my thoughts. That night I finally manage to get some sleep but am tortured by dreams. I'm tortured by the same old dreams of the blonde broken girl who left me behind, who I selfishly ignored. To top it off, my dreams now feature another broken girl, this time a brunette. One, who doesn't remember we met, who I would give anything to help. Her striking blue eyes torment me. In my dreams you can see the suffering within. I think I recognise the signs because I've seen it before. Brokenness. It's what follows me, what I can't outrun. It finds me when I'm awake and then follows me into my sleep. There's no escape. I wake with a jolt. It was a dream. Don't think. Don't think. Don't think!

Blaring noise wakes me from the little sleep I had. I stretch my hand out searching for my phone to silence the wretched noise. Turning off the alarm, I scan my room. My aunt and uncle have provided me with everything I could need. A king size bed, a dresser for my clothes, a flat screen television and a mean sound system that's off the hook. I turn on the stereo, Breaking Benjamin blasting their newest song, and get lost in the beat of the music.

Now it's time to get ready for my first day at my new school. Getting dressed in my newly ironed uniform brings about thoughts of my parents. Every time I started at a new school they would make me pose for an awkward first day of school photo. I guess there won't be any photos this year. Transferring to a new school in my last year of high school was not my idea but theirs. They had the bright idea I needed time away, a change of scenery, distance or whatever lame excuse they could come up with so they wouldn't have to deal with me anymore. Don't think. It's a new day, new school. I don't have time to get lost in my thoughts today. I need to get a move on or I'm going to be late. But first I treat myself to my much needed caffeine hit. When you can't sleep, caffeine becomes a habit; addictive like cocaine. JP hollers at me to hurry so I skull the rest of the frothy goodness and run out to his car where he's waiting.

JP drives us to school in his old, beat up, murky brown Ford. With the windows down, wind whistling past, blowing a breeze into my face I close my eyes and just breathe. And there they are; the piercing blue eyes from the other night. Now they taunt me in my thoughts and in my dreams. Suddenly the car halts and voices penetrate the fleeting peace I had moments ago. Opening my eyes I realise we have arrived at school. So this is it, my new detention centre for the next year. I grab my backpack from the back seat as JP hops out of the car. I follow suit and join him around the front. He doesn't linger in the car park so I follow his footsteps as he leads us up the wide concrete steps. Fist bumping and head nodding to people he knows as we pass on the way.

He leads me to an open door with an older lady sitting behind an antique mahogany desk. Thick wire rimmed glasses frame her plump face. Her hair greying at the sides is pulled back in a tight bun atop her head.

"You alright if I leave you here bro?" JP asks me with a concerned expression. He's been worrying about me since I arrived a few weeks ago and I hate it so I nod.

"Sweet, I'll meet you at lunch time," he tells me before he extends his fist for me to bump, then he's on his way, probably off to find Rafe before classes start. Glancing back at me to make sure I'm okay, I smile at him, letting him know it's alright to leave me. You would think it's my first day of kindergarten and he's my father, the way he's acting. I turn back to the lady behind the desk and she finally notices me and gives me a warm smile.

"Tate Devereaux?" she questions, knowing I must be the new kid.

"That's me," I reply with fake enthusiasm.

"Well come in and let's get you sorted. I'm Mrs. Davies. Head Administrator. If you need help with anything you can come and see me." Her gentle nature puts me at ease and ten minutes later I have my folded schedule in hand and I'm headed to my first class of the day, English.

As I wander to my classroom through the crowded halls I am objectified, like a piece of fresh meat hanging in the tree waiting for the tigers to pounce. The girls all stare at me batting their lashes, not hiding their obvious perusal of me while the guys all eye me up with caution, wondering who the hell I am and if I'm going to be a problem. I'm slightly taller than six foot so I can see why they might be threatened.

I'm relieved when I find the English room. Luckily it wasn't too hard, it was down the corridor from the administration office. I enter the classroom and the first thing I see is her. Tamsyn. She's sitting down the back of the class with some other girls chatting and giggling. Her chocolate coloured waves pulled up into a high ponytail give me a perfect view of her face. I'm drawn to her, her magnet is in full force and I can't stop myself as I squeeze through the aisle of desks to the empty seat in front of her. They all watch me as I approach and try to sit at the empty desk.

"You can't sit there. Seat's taken," one of her friends snidely remarks.

"Oh okay, my bad. Where can I sit?" I query, my eyes locked on hers. Staring straight back at me she wiggles uncomfortably in her seat.

"Up the front with all the other losers. Loser!" she deadpans and it has all her friends snickering behind their hands. She's smiling at me now but it doesn't reach her eyes. Her eyes hold my attention because they are shrouded in pain like it hurt her to say those words to me. The not so friendly smile conflicting with the sadness in her gaze. I plaster on a smile.

"I'm Tate by the way," I say as I turn and walk away to the front of the class. For a second she's confused like she recognises my name. Her drunken memory is probably playing tricks on her with thoughts of deja vu and she can't figure out why my name sounds familiar. Blame the vodka for that, sweetness. I take a seat in the front row of desks and hear the cackling of laughter coming from behind me. I can see why JP described her as cold as ice. She has the persona down pat. It's the wounded spirit inside I want to get to know, not this fake girl she's pretending to be. I angle my head to the back of the class catching her eye. Her laughter seizes instantly and her gaze drops to her desk as she tucks a stray hair behind her ear. The class quietens as our teacher walks in. A short, stocky man with a black receding hairline makes his way behind the teacher's desk.

"Hello class, I'm Mr. Barnes your English teacher for the year and what a year it's going to be." His optimistic attitude has my attention as he goes over the curriculum for the year. You can see why he became an English teacher as he talks about the subject with such passion. English is one of my favourite subjects so I can see this class being one of the highlights of my day. Without realising, the bell rings, signaling the end of class. How time flies when you're having fun. I bend down to pick up my backpack I'd placed on the carpeted floor and pull my schedule out of my pocket. Next up I have Human Biology 101. I lean over to the lanky guy who's sitting next to me and ask him if he can tell me where the science lab is.

"Hey I'm Scott, I've got human bio too. You can walk with me if you want?" He holds out his hand so I extend mine and shake his hand.

"Fitting right in with the other losers there, aren't you?" Tamsyn's friend comments, and the group of girls laugh on their way out the door. Tamsyn walks behind them and avoids my gaze. They don't notice she doesn't join in with their laughter this time.

"Ignore them," Scott tells me, as I watch them exit the class and then follow him. "They're always dishing out crap, thinking they are better than everyone else," he tells me. Sounds like he is used to the way they treat him. We make small talk on the way to the science labs which doesn't take us long. This school is tiny.

As we enter the room for Human Biology 101, a thin framed, middle aged lady stands in front of the class. Her salt and pepper pixie haircut makes her gaunt cheekbones stick out. Her brown eyes are surrounded by a harsh line of black eyeliner. A row of sparkling earrings line her ears from top to bottom. If she wasn't standing there so rigid in a grey pencil suit I would think she was a punk rocker.

"Greetings students," she happily says, as we enter. "I'm Ms. Chadwick for those of you who don't know me. I'll be your human biology teacher for the year. I have assigned seating in alphabetical order so I can learn your names easier. Find your seat and we'll get started."

The bench seats sit two per desk and are pushed together with another so we have four people sitting together in a row. I begin the search for my name at the back of the class and that's when I spot Tamsyn seated at a desk already. So she's in two of my classes. And it's my lucky day, I'm seated right next to her at the end of the row. Before I can say anything to her, Scott comes up on the other side of her where he finds his name.

"Ugh," I hear her quietly groan. She's obviously not happy about being seated between us. I try not to laugh. Karma is a bitch, isn't it?

I glance at Scott before we both sit down and he's thinking the same thing as he has a giant smirk on his face.

Rafe happens to enter the room then and I'm greeted with the biggest smile.

"Yo Tate," he cheerfully greets me as he takes a seat on Scott's other side. He puts his arm along the back of Scott's chair and leans back to get my attention.

"How's your first day going buddy?" he asks.

I shrug as I say, "So-so I guess."

"Well your day has improved now because I'm in class with you," he chuckles, and I can't help but smile. I can see why Rafe is JP's best friend. They grew up down the road from each other and have been best friends since they were little. Rafe is a bit taller than me and built like a brick wall. He spends a lot of time in the gym which explains all the muscle. With his tanned skin, honey brown eyes and brown hair flopping in his eyes, you can see why he has girls hanging off of him twenty-four seven. It's always a different girl too. Doesn't want to limit himself, he likes to say. Feeling better about having a couple familiar people in the class I settle into my seat next to Tamsyn.

Watching her out of the corner of my eye I see her lie her head down on her folded arms like she's going to sleep. Her eyes face the front with a neutral expression so I can't tell if she's interested or not. I shift in my seat and rest my arms on the desk. She doesn't move at all. I glance down at her, she's so tiny and helpless. Turning her head she rests on the other side so her face is away from me and her ponytail hangs down like a curtain hiding her from me. I wonder what she's thinking. Do her thoughts hurt her, like mine hurt me? Or is it something else? Is it a person or situation which has her looking so wounded? How I desperately want to know. I don't know this girl and what I have seen of her, should have me keeping my distance. For some unknown reason she draws me in, like a moth to a flame. Maybe I'm about to get burned.

Don't Think. Just Breathe.

Chapter 2

___________________ Tamsyn ___________________

'm drowning. I'm drowning in pain, hurt and in grief. So overwhelmed I can't think. I am numb. The pain is so strong it's made me numb to everything and everyone. I plaster on my fake smile and do what's expected of me. No one thinks anything is different because I don't give them a reason to. But everything has changed. Why can't they see? Why can't they feel the pain radiating off of me in waves? It's suffocating me. I can't breathe. Why won't they save me? Will someone save me please? Help me, I'm drowning.

Six months ago

As I enter the dimly lit room I feel the chill in the air. Quiet. We all anticipate what we are about to see. A few more steps into the room and I'm glancing down at him. He looks so peaceful. Strangely like himself but strangely different. Eyes closed, lips tightly shut. He could be asleep. But he's not. I watch him closely, waiting for his chest to rise and as I stare at him, I can trick myself into thinking it does. But it doesn't. It's my heart torturing me and my mind playing tricks on me. My cheeks are wet and my vision goes blurry from more tears. I didn't think my heart could hurt more than it already did. Tentatively I stretch out my shaking hand to touch his pale forehead. So cold and hard. It doesn't feel like him. Where has his warmth gone? I run my hands over his chest to get closer to him. Oh how I wish I could hug him and hold him tight in my arms. My shaking hand travels down his arm to his hand. These hard working hands. I try to capture them in my memory so I won't forget these hands. The hands which held mine when we'd cross the road. The same hands which would squeeze me tight when I'd leave. The fingers which would wiggle at the T.V. like it was helping him to focus on the screen better. The hands that worked hard all his life to provide for us. I will truly miss these hands.

So consumed in the moment I don't realise I am alone. Where did they go?

"Oh Daddy how I miss you. I'm sorry I wasn't there. Please come back. I need you back, Daddy." Can he hear my whispers? I can't see now with the river of tears unleashed. Turning around to grab some tissues to wipe my face the door squeaks open and my mum appears. Her face drops when she sees me so distressed.

"Oh love we shouldn't have left you alone in here. Come let's go," she says as she urges me to leave. She wraps her thin arms around me and tries to tug me from the quiet room, away from him.

"No. I want my Daddy," I cry. I plant my feet and won't budge. I'm bigger than her and her efforts won't shift my stubborn feet. "Please, a bit longer?" I plead. She relents and releases me. Eyes back on his chest again in case it rises. I watch and watch. I wonder if he can hear my heart breaking where he is. Can he feel my pain? I cling to his stone cold hand like it will keep him with me. I don't want to let go but I must. I would stay here all day if I could but the others are ready and I don't want to burden them by saying I need more time. Begrudgingly I let go of his hand and bend down to give him a final kiss on his forehead. "Bye Daddy. I love you," I whisper. My feet unwillingly lead me away from him. My heart and head are crying out to go back in there and stay with him but I must go. I must leave. Breathe. Just breathe I tell myself as my feet take me further away from him. My heart cracks more with every step, leaving pieces of me behind in the cold, quiet room. Pieces of myself I don't know how to get back. Pieces which leave me cut open and wounded and I don't know how to stop the pain those wounds cause. I am broken now and I don't know how to fix it.

Present day

I rest my head on my folded arms on the desk and try my best to pay attention to my human bio teacher. Breathe Tam, breathe. You can get through this day. It's one day, you can do it. Stuck sitting between Snotty Scotty and the new guy Tate has me already dreading this class. Why did I have to get stuck between them of all people? Gosh I was such a bitch to Tate in English. Tate. Why does his name sound familiar? Ugh I'm sick of treating people like dirt but I can't help it. He didn't do anything to me and I was a cow. I'm so pathetic and stupid. I need to stop hanging out with those girls. Why do I need to impress them by putting other people down? It's because they don't care about me so they don't see the darkness warring inside of me. I can keep it contained around them. They can't see it leaking out of me because they don't want to see it. No one wants to see because no one cares enough to see. Breathe, just breathe. In and out. In and out. Why would anyone care about me anyway? I'm too messed up inside, too broken to fix.

I glance at the clock on the wall and realise I've been spaced out for most of the class. This is going to be my new normal. I straighten my back and shift to a sitting position so I can pay attention and try to catch the last bit of class. As I'm adjusting myself in my seat my arm grazes against warm flesh. I peer up and notice Tate watching me with a weird expression on his face like he can read my thoughts. Shit, can he read my thoughts? Great, now I'm going crazy thinking the new guy has super powers. Shit Tam, you're cracking now. Why is he still gawking at me?

"You can stop staring at me now," I whisper yell at him angrily trying to get him to break eye contact. His eyes crinkle and his lips curve up then he turns his attention back to the teacher. Jeez, who is this guy? I was a bitch to him in English and here he is smirking at me like he finds me funny. I sit there fuming for the rest of class waiting for the bell to ring so I can get some distance from him. A few minutes later and the bell dings. Quickly I push my chair back, grab my bag and I'm out the door before anyone can stop me. I stomp down the hall and my hands start shaking. I duck into the closest bathroom and lock myself in the last stall. I clench my fists to stop the shaking and notice

I'm breathing hard. What's going on? What's wrong with me? I close my eyes to try and calm down and I'm reminded of bright green eyes smirking at me. Tate. Breathe, just breathe. And it's when I realise... I'm angry. It's the reason I can't catch my breath. I haven't felt anger in a long time since……Before. My heart is pounding. I can't remember the last time I felt it beat or cared for that matter and now it's beating so fast, it's going to rip out of my chest. All because of Tate.

By the time I'm able to calm myself down enough to leave the stall, the bell is ringing for the end of the third period. Shit, I missed my class. I stagger to the mirror and inspect my face. I see hollow eyes lack any life. I see a pale face with sharp cheekbones. I used to have more fat on my face, so I must be losing weight. Guess a lack of appetite will do that to you. My hair is a giant mess. I pull the scrunchie out and brush my hair out with my fingers. Strands of hair come away and I let them fall to the floor. My once thick voluminous hair is thin and lifeless. I try to fluff what hair I have and replace my mask with the fake smile. There she is; the imposter. The face belongs to me but I have no connection with it any more. With this face firmly in place, I make my way to the cafeteria for lunch. I drag my feet to the swinging doors and push my way in, searching the crowded tables for my friends. I line up with a tray to grab some food. Picking up a salad and an apple which I won't eat, I walk to my usual table and take an empty seat. Greeted by smiles, I return one and let them continue their conversation they were having.

Weight across my shoulder draws my attention back to the present. Four sets of eyes are on me and I've got no idea what they want from me.

"Huh?" is all I can say. Laughter comes from my side and I turn to focus on where the weight is coming from. It's Blake's arm, my boyfriend's arm.

"Silly Tammy, you must have zoned out. School boring you already?" he smiles at me. I return his smile like it's the reason I didn't hear what they were saying.

"We were talking about the new guy, JP's cousin and how he's made friends with Snotty Scotty. He must have social suicide if he's hanging out with him," he mockingly comments. "Although he is JP's cousin so can't give him too much of a hard time." Everyone around the table snickers so I join in like I agree. I could add my two cents worth and tell them I'm stuck sitting between Scott and Tate in class but I can't be bothered. I can't wait for this day to be over.

Blake's grip on my shoulder tightens as he pulls me closer into his side. I turn my face to his and turn my lips up into a smile because it's what he expects. A girlfriend should smile at her boyfriend right? She should feel something? But he doesn't take away the numbness. He must believe the smile, leaning forward he brings his lips quickly to mine. I peck him quickly and snuggle into his side. He doesn't know anything is wrong with me. He hasn't noticed a change. You would think being with him for over a year he would see how I've changed. Blake, more than anyone should notice but he doesn't. I don't think he cares. They start talking about plans for this weekend so I zone out again. I'm tired of pretending. I'm tired of trying, tired of being me.

The rest of the day passes in a blur, which I can't remember much of. Next thing I know, I'm getting dropped off at my house by Blake. I lean over the seat and give him a kiss on the cheek.

"See you tomorrow," I say as I exit the car. He beeps the horn as he drives away. He stopped asking me to hang out during the week since I made an excuse my mum needs me home to help her. I walk up to the house and enter the unlocked front door. I find mum sitting in the lounge watching some game show on T.V.

"How was your day love?" she asks without taking her eyes off the screen.

"It was good Mum, I think I'll be able to do better this year," I lie.

"That's good to hear, dear."

"Well I've already got homework so I'll be in my room. Call out when dinner's ready." More lies.

"Okay dear." I trudge up the stairs to my room. Turn the handle and breathe. It's always easier to breathe in here. Dumping my bag by my door I crawl into bed, kicking off my shoes so I can pull my legs up to my chest and hug myself tight. A hug so tight, I hope I can hold myself together by doing it.

"Dinner's ready," Mum yells from the bottom of the stairs. I shake myself out of my brain fuzz and plod downstairs to the kitchen. Glancing at the clock as I enter, I see it's been about three hours since I entered my room and all I did was stare at the wall. I need to get myself out of this funk. Mum has already plated my food so I sit at the table and force myself to eat as I'm not hungry.

"How'd you get on with your work?" Mum asks.

"Good," I reply. Her gaze is on me so I lift my eyes in question.

"You okay dear?"

"Yeah Mum, it's been a long day and I'm tired." Happy with my answer she continues to eat, adding in some commentary about her day. I nod along like I'm paying attention. Piling a spoonful of unappetizing food into my mouth, I excuse myself saying I'm in need of an early night. She lets me go as she clears away the dishes into the sink. As I travel up the winding stairs I think about having a shower but I can't be bothered. I go to my room, strip my uniform off and change into a tank and sleep shorts and snuggle under the covers. I'm so tired. So tired yet sleep doesn't come. I lie in the dark yearning for sleep to take me.

I am two different entities sharing one body. There's the numb person who goes through the motions and does what she needs to, to get through her day. And then there's my soul who's caged and trapped inside me. My soul's screaming out in pain for someone to see me and save me. The numb person has so firmly pushed the caged being down, I fear no one will ever see or hear my silent screams for help. And I don't know how to free her myself, I'm not strong enough. I don't know who I am anymore so how can I free her?

Tate

The rest of the week goes by uneventfully and before I know it, it's Friday. I've gotten into a daily routine riding with JP to and from school then spending most of the afternoon kicking his ass on the Xbox. At night I've been going on runs trying to push my body to its breaking point so it has to sleep to recover. I also have an ulterior motive. I have been keeping up the running hoping luck would be on my side and I might come across Tamsyn again but no luck yet. We share those two classes together so I sneakily watch her out of the corner of my eye every chance I can, trying to observe her. Let's face it, my eyes automatically find her whenever she is near and there's no stopping them. Every day she pretends around her friends she's paying attention and everything is fine but once she gets to human bio she does the same thing. Arms folded on the desk with her head down like she's going to sleep. Staring straight ahead at the board she doesn't move, I don't think she's listening. She doesn't have any of her regular group of friends in this class so it's where all the pretending stops. She can let go of the facade and be herself, her withdrawn, fragile and fading self. She doesn't talk to me or Scott although we don't try and engage with her either. To be honest she doesn't look like she'd hear us if we did. I wonder how I can help her. Thinking about her is another reason I haven't been able to sleep. Worrying about the girl I hardly know. She doesn't acknowledge my presence. I am protective of her and I know nothing about her. Her question echoes in my head. Would you jump in and save me if I was drowning? That begs the question, what could she possibly be drowning from?

On Friday, the last period of the day, I find myself sitting next to her, stealing glances her way, with her in the exact same sleepy position she's taken up all week. The bell is about to ring for the end of the day and I don't want to let her go for the weekend without saying something to her. Feeling brave, I decide to go for it. I don't want to draw attention so I write her a note. Simple. I'm hoping to break through the barrier she projects to the world and embrace the lost girl inside she tries so hard to hide. Thoughts of blonde hair rise to the surface but I choose to focus on the task at hand and my breathing. Don't think. Coming up blank on what to write, I quickly draw a star and shade all around it with my black pen so it stands out. Underneath it, I write the word 'Shine'. I rip the paper off my notebook and fold it up. The bell is about to ring and I don't want it to be awkward when I give it to her. I plan to make a hurried escape out of class as soon as I pass it to her. I pick my bag up off the floor, shove my books and pens into it and rest it on my shoulder. Staring at the clock on the wall, I wait until there's a few more seconds left of the class and grab my chance. With sweating hands I carefully stretch over and slide the folded paper into her open hand lying under her folded arms . The bell goes and I'm off my chair, yelling a hurried goodbye to Scott and Rafe. I'm out the door before she notices what I've done. I hope it gets through to her.

As soon as I'm by myself I take a moment to breathe like Dr. Lawson taught me. Don't think. Don't think. I'm supposed to avoid triggers but I can't resist her. If she does trigger me, it will be worth it to help her, won't it? Don't think, this is a temporary feeling and it will pass, I tell myself. Once I have it under control, I continue towards JP's car and wait for him.

_________________________ Tamsyn _________________________

Lying down in human bio I'm trying to pay attention but struggling to keep focus. It's the same shit, different day. Class can't be much longer, it's gone on forever. Out of nowhere, I feel a small scratch on my palm, the bell rings and Tate's chair goes screeching back on the lino. I sit up and he's up and out the door so quick I barely see his blond head disappear down the hall. He must be in a hurry to get somewhere. Feeling something in my hand, I peel my fingers open and find a piece of folded paper. How did that get there without me noticing? I stay seated in my chair while everyone around me chatters and packs up to head off for their weekend. I unfold the paper to see what it could be. There staring at me is a star. It's been drawn like it's been formed by the darkness surrounding it. Under it, the word 'SHINE'. My breath catches in my throat and my ears block out all sound. Did Tate do this? It must have been, he's the only one who was close enough to slip it into my hand unnoticed. I scan the room and notice it's nearly empty. How long have I been staring at the picture for? I fold it back up and place it in my pocket as I grab my stuff and leave class to find Blake.

Lost in my own thoughts as I walk between cars to get to Blake's car, I feel eyes on me. I scan the car park trying to locate the source. A few cars over to my right I lock eyes with Tate sitting in the passenger seat of JP's car. He's staring at me so intensely like he can see right through me. Shocked by his stare I stand there, glued to the spot. Does he see what I'm trying to hide? Can he feel my pain? I think of the folded paper in my pocket, is he trying to let me know he can see me? How did this stranger see what no one else can? My lips of their own accord lift into a small smile directed at him. An arm around my shoulders brings me out of my trance and I gaze up to see Blake smiling down on me.

"Hey cutie," he says as he delivers a kiss to my temple.

"Hey," I reply distracted, while I'm trying to peek back at Tate. I catch a glimpse of Tate squinting down at his lap with a smile on his face. I wonder if his smile was meant for me but I missed it.

Not long and we are outside my house, and I'm waving goodbye as I walk down the path to my front door. While traipsing inside, I let my mum know I'm home and head up the stairs to my room. I drop my bag, kick off my shoes and flop on the bed. I pull the paper out of my pocket and unfold it. I'm holding the paper tight in my fingers like it's a lifeline, staring at it like it has all the answers in the universe. I have thoughts of stars and darkness, of objects that shine and lastly of green eyes. Vivid green eyes connected to the boy who sees me when no one else does.

_____________ Tamsyn _____________

Monday morning rolls around quickly and I'm distracted by thoughts of Tate while getting ready for school. He consumed my thoughts all weekend. I wonder what he thinks of me and what persuaded him to give me the drawing. Could he possibly see through my facade I show the world? I've stared at the small picture he drew for me all weekend and the edges are a bit frayed now from holding it so tightly. Shine! I don't know where to start with shining. It's the last thing I've had on my mind lately. I've been so consumed by my grief for my dad I haven't let anything else penetrate the haze around me. I've lost myself to my grief and I don't know how to find me again. I don't know if it's possible for me to find her again if I wanted to. She's lost. I'm so far under the waves I don't know how to surface, breaking through to catch a breath here and there then I'm drowning again. I've become so accustomed to this pain, I don't know what it's like to be normal anymore. I can't remember a time when my heart and soul weren't devastated by this grief and hurt. I'm so numb most of the time because I know if I let myself feel, I will get swept away in it. I need an anchor to keep me grounded so I don't lose myself further. It's much easier staying numb.

I'm nervous to see Tate. Will he say anything about the note? Or will he expect me to say something? Okay, nervous is an understatement. I haven't felt anything except numb for so long I've forgotten what anything else feels like. In the space of a few days this guy has made me angry, nervous and if I'm honest a bit nauseous too. How does he do it? He's under my skin. He's awakening parts of me I forgot existed.

'BEEP, BEEP'.

"Crap," Blake's horn beeping disturbs my thoughts and I rush to finish getting ready. Running my fingers through my knotted hair I untangle it the best I can and secure it in a ponytail on the top of my head. Grabbing my school bag off the floor I'm about to leave but remember the drawing. I race to the drawers beside my bed, where I've been keeping it and pull the fragile paper out of my top drawer. Folding it delicately, I place it in my pocket and turn to leave my room. Rushing out of the house I find Blake waiting in his car.

"Hey Tammy, you're extra cute today," he says as he leans in and kisses my cheek as I sit down in the passenger seat.

"Hi Blake, how was your weekend?" I ask him, though I'm not interested in the answer.

"Would have been better if I'd seen you," he replies, smiling at me. "Me, Parker, Chloe and Leyla went to a party." I return his smile not listening to anything else he says. He prattles on without noticing I'm not fully listening. I stare out the window not seeing anything as we pass; it all turns into a blurry mess as we speed past. My mind wanders off these days, not being able to focus on anything, like it's given up and doesn't have the energy to do its job.

Before I know it, we are pulling up to the school car park. Blake puts the car in park and we get out. He wraps his arm around my shoulders and pulls me close to his side as we walk with his bag tossed over his other shoulder. We pass a few other friends on the way into school and Blake chats to them oblivious my mind is somewhere else. My eyes scan the car park searching for the blond boy with the vivid green eyes. I think those eyes are firmly implanted in my brain. At least my brain works sometimes. I don't see him anywhere. Blake is distracted by a conversation with another guy in our year and I make my escape. I get up on tippy toes, give him a light kiss on the cheek signaling goodbye. He quickly turns my way with a smile then is back to his conversation leaving me alone. The bell isn't due to go for another ten minutes so I rush to English in the hopes of seeing Tate.

I enter the empty room and take my usual seat at the back. I must be early if I'm the first one here. That's a first. I pull out my books and pens and set them on my desk waiting impatiently. I start tapping my foot on the floor as the class slowly fills with other students but still no Tate. I glance at the clock on the wall and there are still a couple of minutes before class.

The class is almost full now and my friends arrive and take their seats next to me. Going on about the party from the weekend I nod and smile because it's what they expect me to do. I accidentally knock one of my pens on the floor so I bend down to pick it up and hear the door open. I glance up and there he is. He rushes to his seat at the front of class. The one I made him take on his first day here. Guilt eats at me for the way I treated him on the first day of school. I was mean to him and look at what he's done for me. He's the only one who has noticed something isn't right with me. He has been nice and tried to connect with me through the note. I don't know why he's doing this but I hope he doesn't think I'm a lost cause. Hope, now there's something I haven't felt in a long time.

Fast forward an hour and the bell is ringing. I don't know what went on in class today, I spent most of it staring at the back of Tate's blond head as he and Scott shared a hushed conversation. I wonder what he was saying. I should learn to read lips. Oh my goodness, I wasted a whole class staring at this guy's head. This is so not good. I slowly pack up my things, taking my time because I don't want to walk past him. Please let him leave before me. Man, why am I so awkward? The girls must have said goodbye while I was zoned out because when I finish packing my bag they are gone, along with everyone else including Tate. Phew, at least he's gone now. Thank God for small miracles.

"Shit," I mumble under my breath, remembering it's Monday and I now have human bio where I sit directly next to him. Breathe Tam, breathe. You can do this. Stop acting weird. It'll only be awkward if you make it awkward. I wander to the science lab and take a deep breath before I push open the door. Eyes to the ground I drag my feet to my seat between Tate and Scott who are both already sitting there talking to each other.

"Excuse me," I say, as I pull my seat out. I place my bag on the back of my chair, squeeze onto my seat and shuffle forward. I force myself not to look at them and lay my head down on my arms like usual. I can pretend the note thing didn't happen. My heart beats so loud, I hope he can't hear it. I stare at the board like I'm paying attention but my mind is focussed on the boy who sits so close to me yet is so far away. I don't know anything about this guy and my thoughts have been consumed with him since Friday afternoon. All I can do now is just breathe and try not to let on, he's gotten to me. I've been so numb and closed off for so long now I don't know how to start up a conversation with him. I think it's better if I wait for him to say something. I'm sure he will.

_______________________________Tate_______________________________

A delicate floral essence grabs my attention away from Scotty. Tamsyn. She smells heavenly. How did I not notice her smell before? She squeezes past me into her seat, her skirt brushing against my leg as she sits down. She doesn't acknowledge me at all. She leans down onto her arms, resting her head in her usual pose. I peer at Scott and he shrugs his shoulders like what can you do? I think he's started to notice how spaced-out she is in this class. Her head is turned away from me so I watch her without her catching me. I'm sure she knows the picture was from me as she looked at me in the car. I saw the hint of a smile she had as she stared at me. She must have realised it was me. But she hasn't said anything. I wonder if she will or does she not want to make a big deal out of it? Are her thoughts keeping her from approaching me? I need to persevere and keep trying. I want to connect with her but I don't know how. I don't want to be pushy about it and I don't want to embarrass her. I should wait and see if she talks to me first.

I probed JP with questions about her over the weekend and now he thinks I've got a crush on her. I don't, I want to help her. I'm a total mess at the moment, dating is the last thing on my mind. Girls aren't on my radar. I guess we have something in common, Tamsyn and I are both pretty messed up inside. Well I know I am anyway. Plus she's with Blake. JP said her dad died some time last year but he didn't know much else as he isn't privy to what goes on in her group of friends. It looks like we are both suffering silently.

I could use a friend who knows what I'm going through but I don't want to force it with her. The note was a start. I'll have to see how else I can get her attention. Ms. Chadwick is droning on about our focus in class for the next few weeks. This gives me another chance to study Tamsyn without her noticing. Her magnet is yet again in full force. Her uniform is a couple sizes too big. Her shirt is hanging off her small frame. She doesn't wear makeup I've noticed. She doesn't need it either, she's beautiful without it. She has two sleepers in each of her small ears. Her hair is pulled back into her usual ponytail. It's like she ran her fingers through it then tied it up with little effort.

"Tate?" Ms. Chadwick's voice penetrates my thoughts, and I peer up at her with a guilty face. Shit, did she catch me watching Tamsyn?

"Do you want to come up to the board Tate and fill in the next one?" she asks me, with a knowing smile on her face. Yep, she knows I was being a creeper. Glancing at Tamsyn next to me she still hasn't moved. It's like nothing can pull her away from wherever it is her mind has taken her. I push my chair back with a screech and walk slowly up to the front of the class examining the board as I go, trying to figure out what I was supposed to be learning. There's a skeleton diagram with arrows pointing to different bones and a few already have names. Ms. Chadwick holds out a whiteboard marker for me to take. I'm guessing I have to fill in one of the bones names. "You can pick any one you want to fill in Tate," she tells me.

Studying the diagram, I see a few of the easier ones are already done. I know the breast bone is the sternum so I fill in the line connecting to the middle of the chest in the picture. I click the cap back on and hand the marker to the teacher.

"Good work Tate, nice to see you were paying attention," she smugly says, knowing I was not paying attention. I turn on my heels and shuffle down the aisle to my chair. Tamsyn is still in the exact position I left her in. I guess she won't be approaching me today. I will make it a Friday thing then so I can make my getaway after I slip her a note. We don't have to acknowledge it and it won't be awkward. Feeling better now I have a plan when it comes to her, I settle into my seat and listen to Ms. Chadwick for the rest of the lesson.

The next few days are the same. Tamsyn doesn't acknowledge me and I'm too scared to say anything to her so we go about our days not mentioning the note. It's Wednesday now. The weather is pretty dreary, raindrops pelting down from the heavens so we are stuck indoors most of the day. I usually eat my lunch outside on the benches with JP and Rafe but the weather has made it impossible so I find myself eating in the cafeteria today. I can't help but search for her as I usually only get to see her during our shared classes. The rest of school time we rarely cross paths so I'm excited to watch her interact with her friends. The cafeteria is filled with loud voices and laughter surrounds me. I'm sitting at a table with JP and Rafe. They are talking about some party going down this weekend. I guess they will be trying to drag me along to this party as well. Scott walks by then so I yell out to him to grab his attention. He spots me, smiles and comes my way.

"Hey man, never see you in here. The rain keeping you stuck inside today?" he says.

"Yeah, you wanna join us?" I ask him.

"Sure," he replies, while setting his tray full of food next to me and pulling out the seat to sit down. He exchanges head nods with Rafe and JP gesturing hello and joins in the talk about the upcoming party.

With them distracted, I take a glimpse around the room not looking for anything in particular until I see her. She's seated at a table facing the doors so I have the perfect side view of her. Blake sits on her other side engaged in talk with their friends. They're all talking and laughing and she joins in where she's supposed to but her smiles don't reach her eyes. They're forced. Her laughter stops before the others, like she's laughing for the sake of it. Her elbow leans on the table and she rests her head in her hand, with her fork in her other hand as she pushes her measly salad around on her plate. She hasn't eaten much. A banana lies on her plate untouched. I wonder if she eats at all. Her tiny frame makes me think she doesn't or if she does, it can't be much. She looks so out of place. Like she's an outsider trying to fit in, surrounded but ultimately alone. I know that feeling, I can relate. Why can no one else see the pain she so cleverly disguises?

"So, are you in?" Scott says, while elbowing my arm. I raise my eyebrows at him in question, I don't know what he's talking about. "You know the party on Saturday? Are you going to come with us?" he asks.

JP takes a peek to where I was looking a moment before and a knowing grin takes over his face.

"Are you stalking the Ice Queen now bro?" He laughs at me. The others follow his gaze to see who he's talking about and they join in his laughter.

"You're asking for trouble sniffing around her," Rafe warns me.

"Why?" I question. Three sets of eyes all stare at me. Scott shakes his head before giving his two cents worth.

"Rafe's right. She's trouble man with a capital T. Her group of girls, to put it nicely, are straight up cows. How many times has she talked to you in Human bio?" he asks me. "She's so zoned out in class I don't think she knows what class we are in, let alone, you are sitting next to her. Face it, she doesn't know you exist," he mocks me.

"We won't say anything else bro if you want to try and thaw the Ice Queen but you have been warned, it probably won't happen," JP chimes in.

"Now back to the party dude. Are you in?" Rafe cheerfully asks.

"Yeah okay, count me in," I agree. Happy I'm part of their party group, they start making plans for Saturday night while I steal glances Tamsyn's way without being too obvious. I don't want any more shit from my friends.

Laughter comes from Tamsyn's table. I look up and while they're all laughing, she unzips her skirt pocket sneaking her hand inside. Pulling something out of it, she places it on her lap. It's a piece of paper. She unfolds it and stares down at the paper hidden from view and gets lost in her own little world. She stares at it for a few minutes while everything around her keeps moving. She's so entranced by the paper in her hands. Suddenly Blake turns her way and bumps her making the paper flutter to the floor. I move to get a better view of what could hold her attention so fiercely and I catch a glimpse of a star shrouded by darkness. My breath hitches and eyes widen as she bends to pick it up. It's my star, the one I drew for her. She carefully folds it up and gently places it back in her pocket, zipping it up with the slightest smile on her face. Her eyes gaze up and she catches me staring. Her face transforms. She's doing her best impression of a deer caught in my car's headlights. I don't understand. Why does she think she was doing something wrong? My lip curls up on one side to show her I saw what was on the paper but her face becomes blank and closed off. She turns away from me and back towards her group and doesn't turn my way the rest of the lunch break.

Chapter 5

____________________________Tate____________________________

It's Friday now. The rain has continued to grace us with its presence. Tamsyn is still closed off. She's back to not acknowledging my existence. I thought I made a breakthrough with her when I gave her the note but she hasn't said anything to me about it. And then we had the little incident on Wednesday in the cafeteria. It's like she's embarrassed. She didn't do anything wrong. I don't know. She can be a bit hard to read sometimes. I'm determined not to give up. I won't give up on another person who needs my help. Blonde hair…. Don't think.

Here I am sitting in English listening to Mr. Barnes tell us about our latest homework assignment for the week. We need to come up with a question focussing on education and then use the question as a basis for our essay. We need to provide valid points and debate whether we are for or against the topic. It should be easy enough. I need to think of a question. He gives us the last few minutes to start brainstorming but instead of thinking about English, I think about Her.

It's Friday and human bio is next period, our last class of the day. I need an idea for my note. I've been wracking my brain all week and haven't managed to come up with anything. Well, anything great. I didn't want it too long because I don't want to scare her off with a novel and I want it to have meaning but sometimes less words don't get my point across. I want her to know I see her and what I see is perfect.

She doesn't have to be anyone she isn't and will be accepted for who she is. To me she's more than enough as she is. I've got it. I sit up a bit straighter in my chair and Scott looks at me curiously.

"Have you already figured out what you are going to write your essay on?" he inquires.

"Something like that," I tell him, with a smile in my voice. I'm about to work on my note for her but the bell rings for the end of the period so we start clearing our books away to head to human bio.

Walking down the halls to the science labs I'm lost in my thoughts about her and the note. Will she like this one? I wonder.

"You okay there, Tate? You haven't said anything since we left English and you're starting to freak me out a bit with the goofy grin on your face," Scott teases me.

"What goofy grin?" I deny, as he opens the door to our class. I check my desk and Tamsyn hasn't arrived yet. She must have still been in English when I left, too busy in my head to notice. I place my bag on the floor next to me, pulling out my books and placing them on my desk. I flip to a blank page and get to work on my note.

Out of nowhere I feel Tamsyn's presence like a sixth sense. I gaze at the door as she's walking through it. I'm attuned to her. In my peripheral view I see Scott lean across Tamsyn's side of the desk towards me.

"There's the goofy grin I'm talking about and I've realised what makes it appear," he whispers to me, with a hint of laughter in his voice. I look at him and he nods his head towards Tamsyn who luckily doesn't see our silent conversation. I give him the stink eye hoping he will keep his mouth shut now she's close enough to hear him. He chuckles at me, finding this funny and he sits back in his chair out of Tamsyn's way.

She hooks her bag on the back of her chair, takes out her books and pulls her chair out so she can get in without disturbing me or Scott, scraping the legs of the chair on the ground as she shuffles forward. Wasting no time at all she lays her head on her arms in her favoured position. Ms. Chadwick is explaining the anatomy of the eye. She sets us our work for the class. We are to draw our own versions of the diagram she has on the board of a labelled eye. It gives me a chance to finish the note I was starting in English. I quickly finish it off, going over it a few times in my black pen so it's dark and bold.

Tamsyn has her book angled in front of her so she can still lay on her arms and work, although she rarely works in this class choosing to usually zone out instead. Seeing her participate this time is nice to see. She is taking an interest in this class after all. I try to concentrate on my work quietly while the rest of the class does the same. A peaceful calm surrounds me as I work but inside I'm bubbling with nerves. I wonder what Tamsyn thinks about the last note I gave her. I wish I was braver so I could talk to her. I don't know what to say though. Would she talk back or would she give me the blank stare she's perfected? Ugh when did I become this insecure person who double guesses everything they are going to say? I don't want to say the wrong thing though.....like I did last time.

Lost in my inner ramblings I lose track of time but the bell ringing brings me out of my thoughts and into the present.

"Damn it," I mutter under my breath. I was planning to slip the note to Tamsyn like I did last time but she's already packing up her things. I've missed my chance.

"Tate, you're still coming to the party tomorrow yeah?" Scott asks me, as he's making his way towards the door to leave.

"Yeah, I'll be there," I reply, giving him a fist bump as he passes me.

"Tamsyn, can I see you for a minute?" I hear Ms. Chadwick call out, as the other students empty out of the room. Tamsyn stops packing up, leaving her books on the desk and slides off her chair on the opposite side from me. As she's walking towards Ms. Chadwick's desk at the front of the class, I grab the opportunity to leave my note. I flip to the back of my notebook and tear the page hurriedly out. Placing it on the top of her books, I hastily grab my things not bothering to put them in my bag before speed walking out of the door. I don't risk a backwards glance. Releasing the breath I didn't realise I was holding, I carry on towards the car park where I know JP will be waiting for me.

_______________________ **Tamsyn** _______________________

Come on Tam, you have to start making an effort. You can't keep floating through your days without doing anything. You're falling behind in classes and if you don't start paying attention you're going to fail. You got this girl. You can do it. I give myself a pep talk as I travel from English to human bio not watching where I'm going. Being given an essay question to complete in English threw me off as it's the first big assignment we have had this year, so far. I don't know what I was thinking. Why did I think I could space out in my classes and everything would be peachy? What an idiot. You're so dumb sometimes Tam. Too busy feeling sorry for yourself and now you are getting behind in classes. Oh my gosh, what if I flunk the whole year? Then what will I do? Oh Daddy I wish you were here. At least if you were here this wouldn't be happening. You would be kicking my butt for getting this far behind. Okay I can do this. I can do better for you Daddy. I will do better for you.

My feet have taken me all the way to my human bio desk without me aware of where I was. Great, now I'm spacing out while walking around. This is not what I need, another weird thing to add to my list. Let's hope I never walk into the wrong bathroom. I empty my books onto my desk and move my chair in so I can lean my head down like I always do. Ms. Chadwick is talking about the structure of an eyeball. She tells us to draw the diagram she has on the board. Okay, this seems easy enough. I can do it. I pull my books towards me opening my notebook. It's the second week of school and I don't have one single word written in here. I guess today is as good a start as any. On my brand spanking first page I start drawing my eye diagram. It doesn't look half bad. I find myself enjoying myself and getting lost in my work as the class continues quietly.

Before I know it the bell for the end of the day is ringing. I stare at my work for a second while everyone else is rushing to leave and I am proud of myself for getting it done. It might not be much but it's a start. I slowly get all my things together as I hear Scott ask Tate about a party on the weekend. I pack up slower while waiting with bated breath for Tate's reply. He says he will be there. I wonder whose party it is.

"Tamsyn, can I see you for a minute?" Ms. Chadwick's voice pulls me away from my spying, so I leave my stuff on the desk, dragging my feet towards her. I wonder if I'm in trouble. Does she notice I don't pay attention? I can see in my peripheral view, most of the students have left so at least if she says something embarrassing, no one will be here to witness it.

"Tamsyn, take a seat please," she suggests, holding her hand out in the direction of the seat opposite her. I listen to her advice and sit in the chair waiting to hear what she needs to say. "I hope you don't mind me asking this Tamsyn, but are you okay?" she holds up a hand before I can retaliate. "Hear me out first please?" I nod, since she sounds so sincere. "I've watched you since the first day you came into my class, and in two weeks, today is the first day you have opened your book up. I don't know if you've taken any notes up to this point. You lie down on the desk like you would rather be sleeping than participate in this class. I'm worried about you Tamsyn, you aren't happy when you're in this class. Is there something I can help you with?" she asks kindly.

I can't speak. I don't know how or what to say in response. No one has asked me how I am for so long, I've forgotten what it felt like when someone genuinely cared. My lips tremble and my eyes burn from holding back the tears.

"Awww, it's fine Tamsyn, let it out if you need to," Ms. Chadwick encourages, as she rounds her desk and comes to crouch in front of me. Placing a hand on my knee she waits. Sniffling, I tell her how I'm feeling.

"I've felt so lost lately like I don't know what I'm doing or who I'm supposed to be. My dad died and I'm so heartbroken," I crumble into her arms, letting the flood of tears race down my face as she holds me.

"Let it out, let it all out," she repeats, while rubbing my back and comforting me. I'm not sure how long we stay like that but it's a while. My tears have dried against my skin and my tear ducts have run dry. She loosens her embrace on me, sits back on her heels, looking up at me. "Do you feel any better?" she asks. I nod as my throat is scratchy from crying. "If you ever need anything, you can come to me Tamsyn. I'm here if you need help to catch up in class or if you need someone to listen to and talk to," she tells me supportively. "You did well today in class, I'm proud of you for trying. I want you to try to keep it up from now on. But if you get overwhelmed or life is getting too much, I want you to come to me and we will figure something out. Agreed?" she says, nodding her head.

"Agreed," I reply. Concerned, she asks if I will be okay and I tell her I feel better already.

"Off you go then, and try to enjoy your weekend," she says, as she watches me walk back to get my things.

I grab my bag and books but before leaving I turn to her and I say, "Thanks Miss for listening. I appreciate it." She smiles at me as I leave.

Holding my books tightly to my chest, I race to the car park already late, hoping Blake is still waiting for me. By the time I get there, the car park is almost empty. I must have been in there longer than I thought; the car park is a ghost town. Luckily I spot Blake's car off by itself with him sitting on the hood talking to Parker.

He spots me coming and yells, "There you are, we've been worried. Where have you been?" Both Blake and Parker look at me.

"Sorry I got held up in class," I apologise.

"It's fine cutie. Hop in the car and we'll take you home. Parker is coming over to mine today," he fills me in. I open the passenger side door and hop in my usual seat and Parker sits in the back. Blake and Parker start the conversation up I interrupted as he pulls the car out onto the road.

"So are you free to come to the party with us tomorrow Tam?" Parker asks from behind me. Blake has a quick glance at me eagerly waiting to see what my answer will be.

"Umm sure, I guess so," I agree, nervously trying to sound excited. They both start whooping and hollering making me giggle. I turn to gaze out the window with a smile on my face and realise it wasn't Blake's face which made me agree to the party. It was Tate's and hearing he would be going to a party tomorrow too. I hope it's the same one.

Blake drops me off with a kiss on the cheek and I carry my books inside the house. Mum is in her same spot, vegged out in front of the T.V.

"Hey Mum, how was your day?" I ask, as I head towards the stairs.

"Good dear, how was yours? she asks, without taking her eyes off the screen.

"Good," I reply, as I walk up the stairs away from small talk I can't be bothered with. The door creaks as I enter my room letting my bag fall from my arm to the floor. I walk to my desk by the window and place my books there. The crinkling of paper draws my attention down to my books. There staring at me on a piece of paper are the words 'YOU ARE ENOUGH.' Air catches in my throat as I stare at the bold, black letters. My eyes prick with unshed tears as my shaking hand extends out to pick up the paper. The only conclusion I can come to is Tate. It must be him leaving me another anonymous note. The tears finally reach their tipping point and spill down my cheeks. This sweet boy I hardly acknowledge sees something in me. He sees right into my soul without trying. I've barely said two words to him but he's starting to draw me in and there's no way I can stop it. Can I find the courage to talk to him? If he's going through all this effort to connect with me, the least I can do is make an effort back. I walk to my bedside table, open the top drawer and place his new note inside. Unzipping my skirt pocket, I pull out the now worn piece of paper with the star on it and place it in the drawer alongside Tate's other note. I've carried his note in my pocket all week, wanting to have it close to me wherever I went.

________________________Tate________________________

Riding in JP's car with Rafe and Scott, JP is the sober driver for the night so I'm having a few beers. We have a box to share so I flick the caps off two of them and pass them to the back seat to Rafe and Scott. With the music blaring, we drive to the other side of town to Penny's house where the party is. Apparently her parents travel a lot for work so her house is a frequent spot to party on weekends. Thirty minutes later and we are pulling up to a street lined with cars.

"We'll find a park wherever we can boys and walk over," JP tells us, as he searches the busy street for any vacant spot to park. The street is filled with cars and music thumping from a big white Villa can be heard through our windows.

"Are her parties always this full on?" I ask the guys.

"Yeah, plenty of kids from school turn up here since her parents aren't usually home. It means they can get away with a lot without any chance of consequences," Rafe informs me. "Plus she has a pool and who doesn't enjoy seeing girls get wet at a party?" Rafe adds, chuckling to himself causing JP and Scott to join in with his laughter.

We manage to find a spot about a hundred metres up the road so we park up, skull what is left in our beer bottles and grab the rest of the box to take inside. Meandering down the street, Rafe and Scott walk ahead of me and JP cackling at something Rafe said.

Grabbing my arm, JP asks me, "You okay man? You're a bit quiet tonight."

I slow my stride and turn to JP, "Yeah man I'm fine, you know me, parties aren't my jam."

He throws his arm over my shoulder, "Well tonight you're going to have fun. I'm the sober driver so let loose and enjoy yourself for a bit. Get out of your head for one night. You might be surprised by what happens," he suggests, in a warmhearted tone.

Before I can answer him Rafe twists around with a cheeky gleam in his eyes.

"So are you hoping the Ice Queen is going to be there Tate?" he taunts. JP and Scott snigger along with him.

"Don't call her that man," I defend. "And it's not what you think. I want to be friends with her." This makes them all cackle louder.

"Sure it is Tate. We've all seen the daydreaming look you get on your face when she's around," Scott teases. Suddenly, I grab Scott's shoulders and hold his neck in place to give him a noogie.

"Shut up man," I playfully say, while rubbing my knuckles through his hair. He tries to pull out of my firm grip.

"Don't mess up the hair man," he protests. Letting go we all laugh at him trying to smooth his hair back into place.

Booming music cuts through our comradery as we walk through the gate, up the path towards the craziness. Opening the door, we are blasted with more noise, the music louder inside than expected. The atmosphere mixed with chatter and laughter from all the drunken teenagers makes it hard to think. Following JP, as he pushes through the crowd of people, he leads us to the kitchen where bottles of different alcohol line the bench. Rafe sets our box down and the three of us drinking, take a new bottle, popping the caps off. We all clink our bottles with a united 'Cheers'. I take a big swig of mine, deciding I might need a bit of liquid courage to get me through this night.

We grab another beer each, and with full hands we follow in a line behind JP. He leads us through the house trying to find somewhere quieter where we can chill. We end up going into the back yard where there's more teenagers lingering around. For such a small school there sure are a lot of students.

A permanent bonfire pit is situated in the center of the sparse yard, flames keeping the bystanders warm. Surrounded by sturdy bench seats, it's a popular spot for a lot of people. The pool off to the side already has some people in it splashing each other and fooling around. Wooden pool chairs line one side of it with a few occupied by spectators not brave enough to face the cold water with the chill in the air. I don't blame them. I'm nowhere near drunk enough to get into freezing water, but I guess they can warm themselves by the fire once they exit the pool. It's a pretty sweet set up here; lucky for Penny.

JP leads us to an empty bench seat. We all squish next to each other as we sit. None of us are willing to stand this early in the night. I get stuck on one end next to JP. Inspecting the fire and its surroundings, I see a few people from school I've seen before, including one of the girls who hangs with Tamsyn, Chloe, I think her name is. She's sitting opposite us in a tight black boob tube dress, engrossed in a conversation with a guy I've never seen before. My heart rate picks up, wondering if Tamsyn came with her. A quick glimpse around and I don't see anyone else from their usual group so she must have come by herself.

"Don't make it too obvious you're searching for her," JP teasingly whispers to me, with a smirk on his face.

"Shut up, man," I quietly say, embarrassed I was caught searching for her. Trying to distract myself I drain the rest of the bottle finishing it off and placing it on the grass between my outstretched feet. Popping the cap off the other bottle I have, I skull more beer, trying to get a buzz going. JP is right, I need to get out of my head for a night and forget everything for a while.

"I don't know what it is you see in her if I'm being honest dude," JP states. Annoyed he won't let it go and keeps giving me a hard time, I angle my body so I can look him straight in the eye, deciding to be truthful with him

"Quinn," I deadpan, "Quinn is what I see in her." His eyes bulge and he inhales sharply like I punched him in the gut, unconsciously angling him away from me.

"Shit," he mutters, "Tate, I'm..."

"Don't," I cut him off, and abruptly stand up before he can say anything else. Rafe and Scott notice the tense atmosphere around me and JP and stop their conversation to watch our next moves. "I'm going to go mingle for a bit guys, I'll catch up with you later," I tell them as I drain the rest of my beer and walk away. Don't think. Don't think. Don't think! I tell myself as I push through the back door to the jam packed house propelling myself towards the kitchen. As I approach the kitchen bench I grab two new beer bottles, cramming them in my pockets. I snatch a plastic cup out of the pile and fill it with some bourbon, needing something stronger than beer to take me away from thoughts of her. Don't think. Don't think. Don't think! Peering into the brown liquid, I see a quick flash of blonde hair and green eyes so much like my own. It's the motivation I need as I tip my head back, downing the whole cup. The welcoming burn down my throat warms my stomach and I know soon I'll be free of thoughts of her. I'll be free of everything. Quickly I refill my cup, grab a third beer and turn my back on the bench surveilling the room to see if I recognise anyone. All strangers to me, I release a sigh. I let my feet lead me wherever they want to go, not having a destination in mind.

_______________________ Tamsyn _______________________

It took me hours to find something to wear I was semi happy with.

Nothing I tried on I liked or fit right. I realised I have lost weight because everything in my wardrobe is too big now, hanging off me and not in a good way. Finally I decided to wear my favourite dark blue skinny jeans. They used to fit perfectly but now are so loose, they're baggy jeans. I've paired them with this bright red top you can wear eight ways by tying it differently. It's one of the only tops that would sit nicely on my figure, and with being able to change it, it means I can adjust it more than a normal top. I've got it tied up in a one shoulder top look, which is good. It suits my straightened hair and my makeup. I ride, in anticipation, to the party with Blake, Parker and Leyla. Chloe said she was meeting us there since she's going with Maddox who she has recently started dating from another school.

Approaching the house where the party is, my hands sweat and my heart rate increases. My nerves worsen when I see what most of the other girls are wearing. Most are in skimpy little dresses, hardly covering anything. I've got on a full body suit compared to nearly every girl here. The little bit of confidence I had managed to build up has quickly diminished, leaving me hesitant. I'm wishing I hadn't agreed to come out at all now.

Blake grabs my hand pulling me through the crowd of people inside with Parker and Leyla following. As we arrive at the kitchen where all the alcohol is set up he asks me if I want a drink.

"Something with vodka in it, thanks," I tell him, while I'm preoccupied with searching the overflowing house trying to locate Tate. Searching for him has me anticipating what I will say to him if I see him. I'm not even sure where to start when it comes to him. Blake taps my shoulder, drawing my attention to him as he hands me a plastic cup with red liquid in it.

"Cranberry and vodka," he states. I take a tentative sip to see how strong it is, it tastes a bit tart with a small burn of vodka after I swallow. I may need something stronger later if the party gets too much to handle. I give Blake a small smile in thanks which he returns.

"Let's go find Chloe," Leyla suggests, as Parker hands her a drink he's made for her. Leyla links her arm with me and with drinks in hand, we follow the boys through the house to the back yard. We've been to a lot of Penny's parties before and the bonfire pit is usually one of our favourite spots to occupy. As we exit the back door I feel the chill of the air around me, making me hold on to Leyla a bit tighter for some extra warmth. She leads us to the fire where there's already a few people trying to get warm. The closer we get, the more you can hear raised voices coming from the far side of the fire. Glancing that way I notice it's JP, Rafe and Scott. I can't make out what they are saying from this distance but Rafe and Scott are angry at JP, and JP is waving his hands around explaining something to them. A quick peek let me know Tate isn't with them and my heart sinks a bit.

"Chloe!!" Leyla squeals, turning my head towards the opposite side of the fire where Chloe sits with a fair skinned guy with blue black hair who I assume is Maddox. Pulling me closer to Chloe, Leyla lets go of me to hug her as she jumps up excitedly when she sees us.

"What took you so long to get here?" Chloe questions.

Leaning back from Chloe with a hand on her hip, Leyla confidently says, "It takes time to look this good girl," making her and Chloe giggle. Inspecting them both I notice they look like all the other girls here with tight, body hugging dresses. It makes me feel more out of place than I already did.

Chloe, looking me up and down, hugs me and says, "Tam, you have got to tell me what you are doing to lose weight. You're super skinny. I'm so jealous." I shrug because I don't think she would appreciate me telling her my weight loss is a byproduct of grief and a loss of appetite.

With judging eyes directed at my jeans, she snidely remarks, "You could use some smaller clothes though honey, those do nothing for your figure." As she pinches the excess material at the side of my thigh, I see the hint of a smirk on her face.

"So are you going to introduce us?" I ask Chloe, to get her attention off me. With excitement in her eyes she turns to the guy who was sitting next to her.

"Guys, this is Maddox. Maddox, these are my friends Leyla, Tamsyn, Blake and Parker," she offers, gesturing to each of us in turn. Exchanging hi's and hellos everyone eases into conversations while my eyes wander around in search of Him.

My eyes gravitate towards his friends over the fire and shockingly they are all fixed on me with a range of emotions on their faces. JP glares at me with annoyance, Rafe is amused and Scott is enraged like I have personally offended him. I have no idea why they're all directing these feelings at me but it unnerves me causing me to take a big gulp of my nearly forgotten drink. Shifting my attention back to my group of friends, who haven't noticed my lack of interest in their conversation, I tug on Blake's shirt.

Looking down at me I say to him, "I'm going to get another drink, you want anything?"

"No, I'm okay for now. You want me to come with you? he asks.

"No, I'll be fine. I'm going to head to the bathroom and then grab a drink on my way back," I explain, giving him a kiss on the cheek before leaving. The girls are too engrossed with talking to Maddox, they don't notice me slink away.

Heading back inside to the throng of sweaty, drunk people, I try to push my way through which takes longer than I expect. I'm not the biggest person and nobody can hear my pleas to move over the loud, blasting music. As I'm struggling to make much progress through the crowd, a large, hot hand grips my elbow and a booming "Move," is heard from over my shoulder. I twist my neck to see JP. He tugs me off to the side of the room, the way made clear by people giving him space to get through. I can see the anger pulsing off of him in waves and I'm not sure if it's directed at me or not. I don't know JP well, though we've been through all our high school years together. We have never interacted with the same groups of people. He did ask me out a few years back, before I was with Blake but I blew him off. I staged it in a bitchy way in front of people because Chloe had the biggest crush on him and I didn't want to hurt her by dating him. So I'd hurt him instead. Since then it had always been tense between us so I'd started being cold towards him so he wouldn't pursue me anymore. It did the trick.

Pushing me a bit harshly towards a wall where nobody is, he corners me in by placing his hands on either side of my head, leaning in towards me. I shrink back because his big frame mixed with his rage is starting to scare me.

"What's your game, Tamsyn?" he angrily grunts at me.

"What do you mean?" I stammer.

"Don't play dumb with me. I know you Ice Queen, you've always got some hidden agenda," he snarls at me, using my hated nickname he made for me after I blew him off.

"I don't know what you're talking about, so if you'll excuse me I think I'll be going now," I try to fake a confident attitude but inside I'm terrified of what he might do and want to get away from him. I try to weave my head under his arm restraining me in his cage but he moves it down to block my escape.

"Tate," he hisses at me, through clenched teeth. My heart skips a beat at the mention of his name.

"What about Tate? Is he okay?" My concerned tone throws JP off and his mask of anger drops while he carefully examines me. He straightens up, removing his hands from the wall and instead crosses them over his chest.

"What's your game with Tate?" his tired tone questions me. I can't help but examine him myself. Hiding under his anger I get a big sense of worry from JP. I don't understand why he'd be worried about me and Tate though. We don't talk to each other, unless.....I inhale sharply causing his eyes to narrow at me.

"You know?" I ask him.

"Know what? What's there to know?" I hear the anger returning to his voice.

"The notes," I tell him in a defeated tone, dropping my head to stare at the ground. I had stupidly thought Tate had kept the notes he sent me to himself. It was a private thing between the two of us. Blurry vision alerts me to how much it affects me that he told someone. A single tear slips over the edge, dropping to the wooden floor, my shaking shoulders hunching forward. I wrap my arms around my waist trying to hold myself together until I can get away from JP so I can fall apart in private. A gentle fist under my chin lifts it upwards drawing my tear filled eyes to look at JP. There's no more anger in his eyes, only concern and confusion.

"Sorry, I've upset you, it wasn't my intention. I don't know about any notes. I wanted to warn you away from Tate. He's vulnerable at the moment and doesn't need any more hurt in his life. I've seen the way he's taken an interest in you but you're with Blake. I don't want him getting hurt," he quietly pleads with me. I clear my tears, thankful he doesn't know about the notes. Maybe the notes are a secret between us two. Hopefully they can stay this way. Is Tate hurting as much as I am? I wonder.

"Me and Tate don't talk but if it makes it any better, I promise I won't hurt him," I tell him honestly.

He must see the sincerity on my face as he nods saying, "It's all I'm asking for. Have a good night. " He turns and walks away into the crowd of people I'd forgotten existed for a minute. Making his way easily towards the back door, I let out a breath I didn't realise I was holding and push off the wall needing a drink.

In the kitchen I find a plastic cup and grab one of the vodka bottles filling it halfway then top it off with the cranberry juice. This should do the trick. I take a sip to gage how strong it's going to taste, holding in a cough as my throat burns when I swallow. This will do the trick.

Bringing the cup to my lips I take a bigger gulp this time emptying most of the cup. I quickly finish the rest and grab the liquor and refill my cup with vodka.

"You know if you add a splash of cranberry juice to your vodka, nobody will question why you are trying to get blind drunk." I whip around startled, not realising someone was watching me.

"Thanks," I say to Penny, not commenting on her observation of my drinking habits. Taking her advice, I grab the bottle of cranberry juice and tip in enough to colour it. Glancing at Penny, she raises her cup to me in salute and turns away to go in the opposite direction. With my cup in hand, I merge back into the chaos of people and slowly find my way to the door leading to the back yard, letting the numbness from the vodka settle over me.

With thoughts of finding my friends again, I stumble through the door. As it closes, the blaring music gets trapped inside. The wind whips around my face blowing my straightened hair around. I run my fingers through it wiping it away from my face.

"Shit," I mutter, as I remember I'm wearing makeup, hoping my tears didn't make me look like too much of a mess. Using my index finger I wipe harshly under my eyes to clear away any mascara. Inspecting my finger, I see a speck of black so it can't be too bad and I continue on my way. Laughter and sounds of fun draw my feet towards the pool. There's a few people in there playing volleyball with a net fitted across the center of the pool so I unlock the gate surrounding it to go watch. The gate clicks back into the lock with a bang but no one reacts to my presence, too entranced in their game. I see unoccupied pool seats lining one side of the pool so I stagger towards them planning to hide out here for a bit, instead of trying to pretend I'm enjoying myself with my friends.

As I'm trying to find the perfect spot I catch sight of a lone figure sprawled out on the last chair. They are hidden from view as the lights over the pool miss the corner where they are. It must be why they picked that spot. My feet of their own accord take me closer to the figure, like I'm drawn to them. Something about them is familiar. The washed out blue jeans hug the crossed legs lying in front of them with white sneakers on their feet. A bright red t.shirt hugs their trim form showing off sculpted arms as they rest their hands behind their head. Familiar blond hair sweeps across his forehead and I know stunning green eyes lay hidden beneath his closed lids. Tate. I let out a sigh of relief. Seeing him brings a calm over me I didn't realise I needed. He looks so serene, he could be asleep.

Whether it's my own confidence or the vodka making me brave, I'm not sure but I walk around the side of him, noticing an empty cup and some empty beer bottles down beside his chair. Placing my back towards the pool and squeezing my butt on the chair by his legs, I settle down and stare at him. The squeaking of the chair must alert him to my presence as his body jerks and he opens his eyes. He shakes his head like he doesn't believe I'm real and lowers his arms to his lap.

"Tamsyn?" he asks, unsure.

"Hi Tate," I quietly respond. My voice wakes him up more and his body leans towards me, uncrossing his legs and drawing them up, he plants one on either side of the chair, straddling it.

Looking at me in amazement he responds with, "You're here?" questioning me, his drunken haze filling him with doubt.

"In the flesh," I say, trying to make it less awkward. Leaning closer, he brings his hand up to gently grasp my chin between his thumb and index finger.

"You've been crying," he states the truth, not needing me to confirm it.

"It doesn't matter," I reply. Our eyes locked on each other, we gaze intently into the other's eyes. The noise surrounding us fades into the background, like me and Tate are the only two people here. We sit so still, neither one of us wants to break the trance.

"You look so beautiful tonight," I barely hear him whisper, like he wasn't meant to say it out loud. A faint smile ghosts my lips, which in turn makes him smile so wide like mine was infectious.

Still holding my chin he slowly squeezes as he drags his fingers away reluctant to let go. I miss his touch as soon as it's gone but don't dare ask him to touch me again. What is happening with this guy? I'm with Blake but this sweet guy in front of me draws me in like I'm destined to be near him. There's no point fighting it as it is inevitable. I couldn't fight it if I wanted to.

"What brings you out here by yourself?" I inquire, as it's strange he's out here alone when his friends are at the party too. He doesn't answer at first, he spreads his arm out to grasp my once again forgotten cup.

"May I?" he requests, wrapping his hand around mine to gain access to the cup.

"Sure," I counter, handing over my cup freely. He downs the contents before I've barely let go, hissing between his teeth when the burn hits his throat.

"The water," he supplies. I look at him confused not understanding what he means. His eyes glaze over for a moment like he's remembering something then he shocks me by saying, "You asked me why I was out here. The water is why. I found you by the water before so I thought it might work for me again," he lifts his shoulder in a one armed shrug to say it's not a big deal. He's not making sense now. I wonder how many drinks he's had already because he must be drunk. I've never seen him by water before.

"At first I thought you didn't want to acknowledge you'd met me before, but then I realised you didn't remember me. You were drunk after all. Vodka being your liquor of choice." He tips the empty cup my way to emphasize his point.

I'm still coming up blank, so I ask, "When was this?" Staring at me curiously, he leans back onto the chair and puts his legs straight out on it again in the same position I found him in, except his hands lie in his lap.

He wriggles right to the side away from me saying, "Come lie down next to me and I'll tell you." He invites me with a cheeky grin, patting the space he made clear for me to fit. Gosh he looks so cute right now. All these thoughts cross my mind about how this is a bad idea, what if someone sees us, I'm with Blake, JP said not to hurt him. "Don't think Tamsyn," he says, interrupting the voice in my head, stretching out a hand for me to take, I place mine in his. He pulls me to his side, releasing my hand he puts his back on his lap and I wriggle in next to him. Getting a whiff of a rich, earthy scent I take a bigger inhale, igniting goose bumps on my arms as the smell is all Tate and he smells divine. "Are you cold?" he asks, noticing the obvious goose bumps on my arms. He is way too perceptive sometimes.

"Yeah, a little," I lie, to cover my embarrassment.

"Cuddle in closer to me if you need to, I'll keep you warm," he suggests. So I maneuver myself closer than I already was to him, feeling the warmth coming off his body through our clothes. Being the perfect gentleman in his inebriated state, he keeps his hands in his lap which helps relax me more.

"So, about this encounter we had. Are you going to fill me in now?" I encourage him to talk. He adjusts himself a fraction more so he's comfortable, closes his eyes, and recalls the memory.

"It was a Tuesday night before school started. I couldn't sleep so I went for a run and spotted someone sitting alone at the dock by the water." He's taken all emotions out of his story and is relaying the facts. I don't want to interrupt him so I let him continue.

"It was you, sitting in a green dress. You'd been drinking heavily from what I could tell, so it's probably why you don't remember me. We made introductions then you asked me if I would save you if you were drowning." My sharp intake of breath has him snapping his eyes open to look at me. He rolls onto his side facing me, softly grabs my waist and encourages me to roll onto my side too. We both rest our heads on our hands, but he keeps his other hand firmly holding onto my hip like he's keeping me from running away. Looking into my eyes he asks, "Did you remember?" with hope in his voice.

"No," I softly reply, shaking my head.

"What part shocked you so much, and caused you to draw your breath in?" he quizzes me. I stare at the boy who is a stranger but in so many ways isn't and deliberate whether to bare my soul to him. Trying to give myself more time before I make a decision, I ask him to carry on with the story first. He obliges. "So you asked if I'd save you if you were drowning which got me worried you were going to jump. I told you I would save you and you made me promise. Then you laughed and sprinted away into the night. The next time I saw you was at some party on the Saturday before school started. You were dancing with Leyla and I think you may have seen me but I don't think you recognised me. I was going to come up to you but when I sparked up the courage, you were gone," he states, matter of factly.

Deciding to be honest with this boy who has been helping me, I take a deep breath, keep eye contact with him and confess, "My dad died. It would have been his birthday the day you found me." Understanding crosses his features so I continue. "I didn't know how to deal with anything so I stole a bottle of vodka from my mum's cabinet and drank it in my room. I remember wanting to go to the dock as my dad would take me there when I was younger and I wanted to be closer to him but I don't remember going there or anything. My mind is blank. I remember being in my room but nothing else. It sounds a bit silly saying it out loud." My eyes drop down in embarrassment but Tate's hand leaves my hip, grasping my chin again to bring my eyes back to his.

"It's not silly at all," he softly tells me, while gazing into my eyes. "Do you think you would have jumped in the water though?" He says with a chuckle trying to lighten the mood. Unwanted tears burn my eyes, trying to free themselves from the hold I have on them, trying to keep them contained. Worry shadows Tate's face, "What is it?" he implores, moving his fingers from my chin so his hand can cup my cheek. Warmth is all I feel.

"I don't think I was literally talking about drowning. I meant drowning in here," my shaky voice whispers my secrets, as I point to my temple. It's all it takes for the flood gates to open and tears are streaming uncontrollably down my face as I close my eyes. The warmth leaves my cheek and before I realise what's happening Tate has his arm under my head curling me into him with his other arm wrapping around my torso.

"Sshh, sshh, shh," is all he says, and the tears increase as my hands cling tightly to his shirt and I release all the pain I've kept inside.

I don't know how long we stay wrapped in each other's arms. I drifted off to sleep for a moment which is weird as I usually don't sleep at the best of times. I lift my chin off Tate's chest and his rhythmic breathing tells me he's fast asleep now too. It gives me a few uninterrupted moments to watch him shamelessly. Peaceful is how I would describe him in this moment. He still has a firm grip on me but his face calls to me and I need to touch it. I slide my hand up his chest and timidly place it against his cheek. Mirroring the movement he had done against my face. Scratchy stubble lies under my palm and I find myself running my hand against it, liking the feel. His warm breath caresses my face and I get lost in admiring him. His hair still sweeps across his forehead so I move my fingers to brush it back off his face then return my hand to its original position against his cheek leaving it to rest.

An abrupt, unfamiliar ringing pierces my observation of him but before I can move my hand he awakes. His larger hand is covering mine keeping it firmly planted against him.

The hint of a smile crosses his plump lips, "Don't move, leave it there," he instructs. How long was he awake for? My cheeks heat with embarrassment at being caught. As he lets go I obey and leave my hand against his stubbly cheek while he digs in his back, jeans pocket to locate the noise. Opening his eyes, phone in hand, he swipes up to answer the call, placing it by his ear. His eyes bore into mine, with the smile still evident on his face as he leans his head into my touch. Not knowing who is on the other end, all I hear are Tate's answers to his caller.

"Yeah I'm still here." "I'm by the pool." "It's forgotten man, don't sweat it". "No, I'm with a friend," at his response, a full smile takes over his face. "Don't be nosey," he tells his caller. He's quiet for a moment while the other person talks then he replies with, "Ok, I'll meet you there soon." While looking at me something clicks in his head and he says, "Ah JP hold on a sec." He brings the phone down to his leg and holds it against his thigh so JP can't hear what he's about to say to me. His face transforms to one of sorrow with his smile being replaced with a frown. "Who did you come to the party with?" he sadly asks. Knocking me back to reality, I remember Blake and try to remove my hand but his defeated eyes plead with me. "Leave it there, please?" I indulge his request by keeping it there. I run my palm against his stubble once more and he closes his eyes enjoying my touch. With closed eyes he asks me, "Do you want me to ask JP if Blake and your friends are still here or do you want us to take you home?" He didn't need me to confirm I came with Blake, he already knew. Shit, I don't want to hurt him but if I don't find Blake I'll have to explain to him where I went.

"Blake if it's okay, please?" I softly reply. Slowly opening his strained eyes he holds my gaze, lifting the phone back to his ear to talk to JP.

"Sorry about that man. Can you tell me if Blake is still around?" Never taking his eyes off me he listens to JP talk. The longer he talks the more agitated Tate gets. His muscles tense and his jaw clenches under my hand. His once relaxed breath becomes heavy. "Take his keys man. He doesn't sound fit to drive," he snaps into the phone. "Tell them sleep it off here and we will get Tamsyn safely home for them." Ugh I guess Blake got wasted after I left him. "Sort it JP, then come find us at the pool so we can leave," he demands, before hanging up and shoving his phone roughly into his back pocket.

______________________________________Tate______________________________________

I'm fuming at Blake. How could he be so reckless and drink way too much when he's supposed to be driving Tamsyn home? Her tiny hand still rests on my face where I've asked her to keep it. I know when she moves it away, our moment will be broken and I selfishly want to stay with her like this for as long as I can. JP has the fun job of telling Blake we are going to take Tamsyn home. I'm not sure how it will go down but I could care less about Blake's feelings at this point. Her girlfriends have disappeared too, both leaving a while ago with the guy I saw Chloe with. I don't know if they checked in with Tamsyn to see if she was okay. She has been with me for a while and no one came here looking for her. What useless friends. It's a lot quieter now so I assume most people have gone home.

"You okay in there? You're lost in thought?" she asks in her caring voice, drawing my attention back to her.

"Yeah I'm more than okay," I admit, squeezing her tighter in my arms, drawing her closer to me. After drifting off I've sobered up a bit but I wish I'd had less to drink tonight so I could remember every detail about her. Having her here in my arms now is incredible. She releases my face, drawing her hand down my body and wrapping it around my waist pulling me closer to her. She must want the contact as much as I do. Resting her head on my chest she sighs and it's the sweetest sound like she's content being in my arms. I can't help myself; I nuzzle my nose into her bare neck and breathe deeply, taking in her heavenly scent. Now I know the smell associated with her, I can't get enough.

"Did you sniff me?" she questions me, as she giggles into my chest.

"Yes I did. You smell so good," I tell her unashamedly.

The slamming of the pool gate has me craning my neck around to see who it is. Tamsyn burrows her head into my chest, concealing herself from view.

"It's only JP," I quietly tell her, and she lifts her head up. He waits a few chairs away with his back to us to give us privacy. We focus on each other, both not wanting to move but knowing we have to. I stretch my hand out and push the hair away from her face with my finger. Moving my hand to the base of her neck I lean in and press a long kiss to her forehead. Pulling away slowly, I glance down at her and her eyes are closed with the smallest of smiles on her face.

Reluctantly, I loosen my grip on her and whisper, "Come on, let's get you home." We both simultaneously turn our opposite ways and get off the chair. Having been lying down for so long on a wooden chair I'm a bit sore and stiff so I stretch my arms above my head to loosen up a bit. I extend my hand out to her which she happily takes not needing any coaxing from me. Hand in hand we stumble towards JP, the liquor still running through my system making me a tad wobbly. JP turns toward us when he hears us approaching, his eyes widening when he sees our connected hands. Tamsyn notices his intent stare and tries to pull away but I tighten my grip not wanting to lose the contact already.

Hoping to distract her, I ask JP, "What happened with Blake?"

He lets out a sigh saying, "He's drunk bro, like super wasted. I don't know why he drove if he was going to drink like he did. And Parker isn't much better off. I told him I'd seen Tamsyn looking for the girls but they'd left so I would take her home for him," he explains to us.

Me and Tamsyn must both look at JP guiltily before he adds, "Don't worry, your name didn't come into it bro and he was happy Tamsyn had someone she knew taking her home. He laid down on the couch a minute before I came out here but he was already snoring away," he says, easing my worries. "Let's sneak out the side gate to be safe so he doesn't see her if you're worried," he suggests.

"Good idea," I agree and we follow JP as he leads the way.

As we approach the wooden gate attached to the side of the house, JP stretches up to unlatch the hook quietly, in case anyone is still around. The house is a complete contrast to the one I arrived at earlier in the night. The temperature has dropped considerably and Tamsyn shivers next to me.

"We will turn the heat up in the car for you," I tell her, giving her soft hand a gentle squeeze. Secretly, we proceed through the gate and round the side of the house by some bushes, heading out onto the road unseen.

Remembering I came with more people, I ask JP, "Where are Rafe and Scott?" Snorting, he slows his stride to walk beside us to talk.

"You two missed out on the action. Scott drank too much, he ended up puking way too close to the bonfire. I took him to the car to sleep it off. Then I came back and Rafe was hitting on a random girl whose boyfriend wasn't too impressed so I ended up dragging him to the car to save him from himself. It took me longer than I thought to get Rafe to stay in the car then I came looking for you," he informs us, finding it humourous. As we trudge our way through the now empty street to the car I keep ahold of Tamsyn's hand. It's like her hand was made for me. Arriving at the car, I can see Scott's head pressed against the rear, side window.

"Rafe's in the front. You two can squeeze in the back," JP informs us, so I drag Tamsyn around to the other side of the car so we can get in. Opening the door, I pop my head in and see Scott sprawled out diagonally taking up space in the middle. I hop in and push his legs towards the opposite door. He answers me with a couple of grunts then is back to snoring. Tamsyn follows me in. She's so small, she hardly takes up any room which is good because me and Scott's tall frames take up more than the average sized person. We buckle in, JP starts the car and we're on our way.

As we start our journey back to the other side of town, I ask JP to turn the heat up for Tamsyn. Her thin frame contains hardly any fat, so no wonder she's shivering considerably. I lift my arm over her small shoulders and pull her into my side. Her body is tense, not relaxed like she was when we were at the pool. I peek down at her and her eyes are watching JP. Is it him making her nervous? Giving her a slight shake to gain her attention, I raise my brows in a quizzical look. She returns it with a small shake of the head which I take as meaning not to worry about it. I beam at her hoping it will relax her and try again to pull her in closer to my side. This time she doesn't resist and wraps her arm around my waist, snuggling her head onto my chest. Her touch soothes me in a way I didn't know was possible. I relax, closing my eyes to rest.

"Come on bro," I hear JP whisper yell to the side of me. I twist my sleepy head towards his voice and see him at the open car door trying to pull Scott out. Warmth at my side brings my attention to it and there lies a peaceful angel fast asleep. Her face is free from worry, without a care in the world. I wish she could look this untroubled all the time.

"A little help would be nice if you're awake bro," JP's strained voice cuts through my ogling, and I remove my arm from around her. I position her so her head rests against the door so I can help JP and she can sleep uninterrupted. Once she's settled I turn my focus to JP. He's trying to pull Scott out by his arms, but Scott's dead weight is too heavy for him alone.

"I'll push him out from here. Get ready to catch him while I get out," I tell him. JP leans in closer putting his hands under Scott's underarms.

"Hurry, he smells like vomit." I use all the strength I can muster and push Scott's back so he's forced into JP's hold. It works and JP drags Scott from the car. I unclip my belt and hurriedly exit behind him, grabbing one of Scott's arms and throw it over my shoulder. We half drag carry Scott up the path to his front door.

"How are we going to get him inside man?" I whisper to JP.

"Search him for keys," he replies. We juggle to hold him up while we pat his pockets down with our free hands.

"Here, think I've found some," I tell JP, as my hand makes contact with metal in his front pocket. Pulling out the keys, I hand them to JP so he can try them in the lock. The second one he tries works and we stumble clumsily inside. "Put him on the couch," I tell JP, knowing his parents were away for the weekend so no one will see him passed out drunk there. We flop him down and then I wrestle his head down on the pillow with him facing sideways in case he spews again. JP lifts his feet onto the end of the couch so he's in a more comfortable position. JP places Scott's keys on the hallway table on our way out and we flick the lock before closing the door behind us.

"What a night. Remind me it's someone else's turn to be the sober driver next time," JP tells me, as we shuffle back to the car. Getting back into our seats, Rafe and Tamsyn haven't moved, both out for the count. "Now for drunken master number two?" JP asks me, with a chuckle knowing I want as much time with Tamsyn as I can get, even though Rafe and JP live on the same street. We pull up to Rafe's house and because JP is probably used to waking a drunken Rafe up he gives his arm a giant shake.

"Wakey, wakey bro, time to go," he tells him, in a sing-song voice. He gives him a few more heavy shakes and Rafe stirs. "Come on, wake up," Rafe slowly wakes up, his heavy lids opening to look at JP.

"We home dude?" he sleepily asks him.

"Yep, time for you to go bro. I'll see you tomorrow. You need a hand?" JP asks, unsure how awake Rafe is.

"Nah, I'm good," Rafe assures him, holding out his fist to bump first to JP then turns to me doing the same. I lean forward between the seats hoping to keep his sight off Tamsyn who's still sleeping soundlessly in the back. He clumsily unclips his seat belt, opens his door and swings his legs out first. Slowly, lifting himself to standing he steadies himself before he walks the short distance to his door. We wait until he enters before JP pulls away from his house.

"Do you know where her house is or do you need me to wake her?" I softly ask JP, trying not to disturb Tamsyn if I don't have to.

"Let her sleep bro, I know where she lives," he assures me, and drives confidently in the direction of her house. I have no idea where she lives so I'm glad he does. I take in her tranquil face while I can. Her soft features look different when she isn't haunted with her regular thoughts tormenting her. Will tonight change anything between us or will she go back to ignoring my existence once we are back at school? Will she pretend like tonight never happened? In case this is the way things play out on Monday, I want to get my fill of her before she goes. I want to see her so I run my finger across her temple, sweeping the loose hair behind her ear. She sighs, even in her deep slumber she can feel my touch. With that sound alone, she pieces back together a crack in my fractured heart.

Too soon and JP is pulling to a stop.

"This is her place," he says, staring at the picture perfect house before us. A white picket fence frames the yard with a stone path leading to a wide wraparound porch. A new modern two storey house towers before us. The house is all white except for grey shutters and a darker grey porch. It's the house I would have pictured her living in.

Breaking up my thoughts and my admiration of her house, JP sadly says, "You're going to have to wake her and let her go bro." Like he knows this is the end of our rendezvous. Letting out a huff, I reluctantly lean towards her to shake her arm gently.

"Tamsyn, you're home now. Wake up," I try to coax her out of her dreams. She rolls away from the window towards me and cuddles into me.

"Hmmm Tate," she sighs, while still fast asleep. My heart stops, eyes widen and I look at JP who is quietly sniggering behind his hand.

"Guess you made quite the impression," he quietly laughs. With a giant smile on my face I lean forward and playfully punch his arm.

"I'll carry her to the door, she should wake up when she's outside," I suggest to JP. "Can you get the door man?" I ask him. He jumps out and opens my door for me. I wrap an arm around Tamsyn's back and then scoop her legs up with the other. With her in my lap, I shuffle to the open door and slide out. Standing up, I carry her effortlessly as she is feather light. She needs to put a bit of weight on. A slight breeze could knock her over. Trying not to jostle her as I walk up the path, I hold her tightly to my chest. I bend my head to take one last sneaky sniff of her enticing scent and nuzzle her neck again which is easily becoming a favourite spot of mine.

As I get to her porch, I place her feet down while I stand on the path so we are closer in height.

"Tamsyn," I call to her, trying to wake her. Her sleepy eyes finally peel open taking me in.

"Hi," she shyly says, as she wakes up more.

"Hi," I say back. "You're home now," I inform her, and she looks behind her recognising her house.

"Thank you," she quietly says, rubbing the sleep from her eyes.

"You're welcome," I tell her, with a smile on my face. "I better go, JP is waiting at the car," I wistfully tell her. Her face drops, her bottom lip has a slight tremble and she hugs her arms around her waist.

"You okay?" I quickly ask, worried.

"Yeah, I'm okay, I should probably get some more sleep," she says, trying to act like everything is fine.

I see through it but I don't want to push her so instead I say, "Okay then. Goodnight Tamsyn," and I start walking backwards slowly.

With a shaking voice she turns and whispers, "Goodnight Tate." I halt watching her slow steps towards her door. She reaches her hand out to turn the knob but then has second thoughts and twists around knocking the air from my lungs. Her face is wet from tears streaming down her face and without thinking my feet are speeding towards her with outstretched arms. When I'm within reach she leaps into my embrace, wrapping her thin arms around my neck holding on so tight, like she's scared she might blow away. Her legs automatically wrap around my waist. My arms enfold her to me as I run one hand down her head trying to soothe her.

"Shh it's okay. Shh, shh, shh," I soothingly say. I turn around and see JP get out of his car with a worried expression. I hold a hand up to him so he knows to give us a minute and he hops back in the car closing his door quietly. I sit down on the top porch step, with Tamsyn wrapped around me, her wet sobs soaking my shirt. I try to comfort her by stroking her head letting her know it's okay. "I've got you. You're alright," I reassure her as I gently rock her in my arms. Her whimpers quieten and I release my hold on her to place a hand on each side of her head, gently forcing her to look at me.

"What's wrong?" I ask, staring at her tear stained cheeks. She looks so miserable, with her eyes looking down. "We're friends now aren't we?" I try to cheerfully ask her. Staring at me she nods with a faint smile. "Well friend, I'm not going anywhere. If you need me for anything I'm here. Got it?" I firmly tell her.

"Got it," she softly replies.

"Are you going to be alright this time?" I question her.

"I'll be fine now," she reassures me, as she lets go and unhooks her legs from me. Placing her hands on my shoulders, she places one leg on the step and swings the other leg over me to stand.

I follow suit and stand in front of her then say, "In you go this time." She smiles at me one last time as she turns her back to me. She hurries to the door like she might change her mind if she hesitates, opens it and is inside before I know it, closing the door behind her.

I drag my feet to the car, glancing back at her house a couple of times in case she comes back out. Opening the passenger door, I hop into the seat next to JP.

"She alright?" his concerned tone has me turning to look at him.

"I hope so man. She may appear like an Ice Queen to you but she's not. Could you try to put your previous perceptions of her to the side for me please?" I plead with him. He studies me for a bit before he answers.

"Sure. For you, I can do that," he says, holding out his fist for me to bump. He starts the car and pulls away from her house and I look back one more time before it is out of view.

Silence fills the air for a moment before JP can't help himself by saying, "Let me say one thing bro, then I won't say anything about her again." I nod at him letting him know to proceed.

"She's with Blake. They've been together for a year. I don't want you getting your hopes up, thinking she will magically break up with him and run into your arms. I want you to be prepared in case it doesn't go the way you're hoping for. I've said my piece. I won't say anything else." I let his words soak in, knowing he's right. It is a lot to expect her to break up with him and run to me. To choose me, who she's known a short while, over someone she's been in a relationship with for a year. Anyway, we are both so messed up. I don't think it would be good for either of us to get into a relationship right now. Friends are all we can be, I've decided. There's no way I can go back to how we were before tonight so friends will have to suffice.

"I want to be her friend, man. That's all. Just friends," I try to convince JP, as he parks in our driveway.

"Whatever you say," he replies, in an unconvinced voice.

"Fine, I admit I want to be for her what I couldn't be for Quinn. I can't let history repeat itself." He doesn't respond, I don't think he knows what to say. We head inside to the quiet house. As we open the front door, JP taps me on the shoulder.

"Anytime, you want to talk about Quinn, I'll listen."

"Thanks, man," I say, and go to my room. I pull my phone from my back pocket to check the time. It's nearly four in the morning and I'm exhausted. Kicking my shoes off, I unbuckle my jeans and drag them off throwing them in the corner. I grab the hem of my shirt and pull it over my head but catch a whiff of Tamsyn's lingering scent. Letting go, I scrunch the front of my shirt and lift it to my nose for another smell. Taking a deep inhale and closing my eyes, it's like she's in the room with me. I decide to leave the shirt on and sleep in it. I switch on my bedside lamp; turn my room light off and then pull back the blankets and slide into bed, covering myself. I flick the lamp off and I'm cloaked in darkness. I breathe in deeply of my new favourite scent, and it's with thoughts of Tamsyn in my arms I manage to lull myself into a dreamless sleep. For the first time in a long while, I sleep without haunted memories and am at peace.

Tate

Sunday passed uneventfully. I did manage to figure out where to start with my English assignment so it was productive at least. Later in the day JP and I lay around on the couches playing on the Xbox. It helped take my mind off Tamsyn for a while but thoughts kept creeping in. I wondered what she was doing and how she felt about Saturday night. Did it mean as much to her as it did to me? I'm an idiot, I should have asked her for her digits then I could have set my mind at ease. I couldn't wait to see her on Monday and anticipated what she would do. Are we friends now? All these unanswered questions plagued my mind.

When I arrive at English Monday morning, she is already seated in her usual spot at the back. I walk in and can't help but look at her. She doesn't see me enter as her focus is directed out the window. Her friends are busy laughing with each other to notice her lack of interest in their conversation.

"Hey man," I greet Scott.

"Hey," he replies, a bit more sullen than his usual chipper self.

"You good?" I ask.

"Still getting over my hangover. I'm never drinking again. Can't remember half the night. I didn't do anything stupid, did I?" he cautiously asks.

"You threw up next to the bonfire pit and had to be dragged in your house by JP and I. Otherwise, I think you were fine," I tell him, laughing at his horrified expression.

Hanging his head in his hands he mumbles, "I'm never drinking again." I pat him on the back, chuckling at his somber mood. Class begins and brings both our thoughts back to English instead of worrying about Saturday.

I get held up by Mr. Barnes after class, asking him for help with our essay question so when I walk into human bio, class had already started. I apologise to Ms. Chadwick as I enter. Hurriedly, I take my seat and notice something is off with Tamsyn today. She's not lying down on her desk like she usually does. She's agitated. Her right foot is tapping her chair making her leg shake. She's restless in her seat, wriggling every so often like she's trying to get comfortable but can't. She's tapping her fingers on her thigh. What has got her so strung out? She's extremely focussed on something at the front of the class, she doesn't notice me blatantly watching her. I take my focus off Tamsyn and glance in the same direction as she is. At the front of the class, there's a couple of eyeballs in a glass container with 'Dissection' written on the board behind them.

It must be the eyeballs causing her to get worked up. As Ms. Chadwick continues talking, Tamsyn becomes more agitated. We are going to be discussing cow eye dissection today. Her leg is now shaking uncontrollably with her hand tapping in rhythm on her thigh. I want to calm her down so I instinctively grab her wrist on her thigh to stop her. She jolts from my touch and looks at my hand wrapped around her tiny wrist.

"Breathe Tamsyn, it's okay. I'm here," I whisper, so only she can hear. She visibly draws a breath into her lungs and raises her head to look at me. Pain is all I see. How can I take her pain away? "Don't think

Tamsyn, it's what I do. Don't think," I whisper my motto to her. "Turn your brain off, push it aside and don't think."

"Don't think," she repeats, as she slows her breathing. After a couple minutes of her being more relaxed, I ease my grip on her wrist and break contact but startle her and she grabs my hand in hers. "Could you hold on a bit longer?" she pleads, her voice laced with sadness.

"Sure I can," I say, softly smiling at her. I lace my fingers through her soft ones and hold her tiny hand in mine and move our hands against my thigh instead. I've calmed her down but her tight grip never softens. I think it's her way of letting me know she's not ready for me to let go yet. I'm fine with that. I cling to her hand and comfort her. I run my thumb back and forth over the back of her hand to try and calm her some more. Our hands safely hidden from view under the desk, no one else knows what's going on except us. It's nice to be in a bubble with her. And this is how we stay for the rest of the class. Tamsyn clinging to me like an anchor to keep her grounded and me selfishly not wanting to let go because when I do, the moment will be lost... like she is.

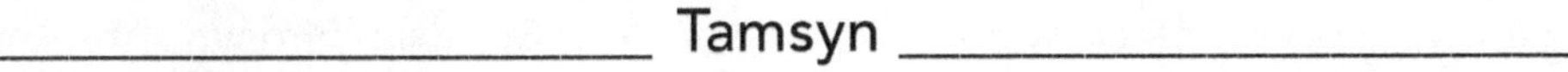

Tamsyn

His blue lifeless eyes. It's all I see. I shudder. Seeing them took me back to the moment when I found him. I'd come home late from school, hanging out with Blake like I usually did after school. We were always too busy making out in his car to care about the time. As soon as I opened the door, it's like my body could sense something was wrong. The hairs on my arms stood up sending a chill up my back. It was Thursday so my mum was working late at the office which wasn't unusual. It meant she wouldn't be home until late. Something in the air felt off though. Like the house was too quiet.

"Dad?" I called out. No answer so I walked down the hall to the kitchen. At first I didn't see him, but feet sticking out behind the kitchen bench caught my eye. I ran to him and he's slumped on his side. I shake him but he doesn't answer me. "Daddy?" I plead with tears streaming down my face. I grab the home phone to call an ambulance and as the operator talks to me over the phone I stare at his blue unseeing eyes, and can tell there is no life left behind them.

A hot grip on my wrist brings me out of my trance and I'm back in human bio. My eyes find the source of heat and follow it upwards until I'm staring at concerned green eyes. Tate has a worried look on his face. He tells me to breathe. I can do that. I inhale deeply not realising I must have been holding my breath.

"Don't think Tamsyn, it's what I do. Don't think," he whispers. It's what he does? Does he know something about my pain? He instructs me on what to do so I push the thoughts aside and focus on Tate instead.

"Don't think," I repeat. I stare at his emerald eyes and slow my breathing by studying his face. He has thick brows framing his eyes and are a couple shades darker than his light hair. Furrows on his forehead lead down to a crooked nose like it's been broken before. Soft lips with the bottom lip hanging out a bit more in worry. His sculpted jaw makes his pointed chin stick out, with a dimple right in the middle of it. I'd never noticed these things about him before. Breathe Tamsyn, breathe I tell myself.

His grip on my wrist loosens and I get a flash of blue eyes so I grab hold of him tighter. I must look crazy to him but I beg him to hold on a bit longer as his touch keeps the thoughts away.

"Sure, I can," he softly replies, smiling sweetly at me. With our fingers intertwined, he rests them on his thigh while his thumb absently strokes my hand. I focus on the strokes, repeating don't think to myself and it's how we stay for the rest of the class.

The ringing of the bell alerts me to the end of class. Ms. Chadwick lectured today and we were supposed to take notes. I didn't want to let go of Tate's hand so I didn't get anything written down.

"Tomorrow we will pair up and start the practical part of the dissection and put our theory work to use so I hope you were listening today," she tells us. Tate tugs my hand and I turn to face him. We are both still seated at our desk while everyone around us is packing up.

"Hey Tate, you coming man?" Rafe calls from the doorway, where he's waiting with Scott.

"I'll meet you guys there," he yells back, turning to give them his attention. I look at the guys and they both glance at me, smiling they nod at Tate like they have some inside joke and walk away.

"You okay now?" Tate kindly asks me

"Yeah. Sorry. The eyeballs triggered something," I explain, while staring at the desk, not able to look him in the eye.

"You don't have to apologise for anything. I'm glad I was here to help. I'm happy to lend my hand any time you need it," he says, lightly chuckling. I look up into his eyes and see the sincerity on his face and can't help but smile back. Warm strokes glide across the back of my hand and it's then I realise we are still holding hands. I freeze and he must see something on my face as he looks worried again.

"Tamsyn, don't freak out. I'm going to let go of your hand now," he says. I nod and he gently peels my tight grip away from his hand. I didn't realise I was holding onto him so fiercely. Weird. I feel the loss of contact instantly, like he took all the warmth in the room with him. I wonder if he feels it too?

"Are you gonna be alright? Do you need me to walk you somewhere?" he asks me. I stare at him blankly, trying to remember what day it is and what I have next.

"What period is it now?" I ask him, having lost track of time.

"It's third period now. Do you need me to take you? What have you got?"

He's concerned again and I don't want to bother him so I say, "No, it's okay, I'm gonna get myself together a bit and then I'll go. You can head off to your class now Tate. Honestly, I'll be fine. I'm a big girl."

"If you're sure?" he questions, with the worried look still on his face.

"Yeah go ahead. I won't be too far behind," I tell him encouragingly, so he will go. He packs up his things, picking up his bag from the floor and putting his books into it. I place a big, fake smile on my face to show him I'm recovered and he returns it with a small smile of his own.

"See you later, Tamsyn," he adds as he walks towards the door to leave.

"Tate?" I call out to him, making him turn around. He raises his eyebrows in question. "If we are doing the dissection tomorrow, could I, umm, borrow your hand again if I need it?" I suggest. Suddenly, his face transforms into the happiest I've ever seen him.

Beaming at me, he answers, "Anything you need Sweetness, I'm here." And with that he swiftly opens the door and rushes off to class. Leaving me to ponder about the fact he called me 'Sweetness'. I find my smile now isn't so fake; it's the first genuine one in a while.

I'm still shaken up so I collect my things slowly. There isn't a class in here this period so I'm not rushed out of the room but I'm still not ready to go to my next period either. I glimpse at the clock on my way out and see I've already missed a quarter of the class. If I enter now, I'll have to get a late slip so I might as well not go to class at all. Trekking down the quiet hall, I come to my new sanctuary which I use when I need to pull myself together. Pushing open the bathroom door, I check it's empty. Dragging my feet to the last stall I enter, locking the door behind me. I hang my bag up on the hook, close the toilet lid and sit down pulling my legs up into my chest, hugging them tightly. Now all alone and unseen I fall apart. I let the images of my dad's lifeless body pound into my head. There's glimpses of him laughing and smiling but my mind always reverts back to when I found him lifeless on the floor. It's the image that haunts me the most.

My overwhelming heartache consumes me in my quiet hiding place. My heart wrenching sobs are all that can be heard around me. I let it all out in hopes it will leave a void inside. I want to be numb again. I don't want to feel. Lately the floodgates have been smashed open and I'm crying at every turn. Pressing the sides of my head with my palms trying to squeeze the images out of my mind doesn't work. It's getting harder to turn my numb switch on. My switch has started to glitch and I can't control my emotions like I could before. They're pushing to the surface, trying to get free and I'm struggling to keep them contained. Breathe, just breathe. I try to calm myself down but my sobs turn into blubbering hiccups. Focussing on my breath is not working. I will need to try something else. I hastily unzip my pocket, searching for what I need. Grasping it between my fingers I pull it out, unfolding it. There, staring at me is my star. Welcome thoughts of the boy who gave it to me fill my mind instead and slowly I am able to calm down. His bright green eyes, and lips turned up with perfect teeth, showing in a brilliant smile replace my tormenting thoughts. 'Sweetness' it's what he'd called me. I focus on him and my heart is lighter.

The lunchtime bell will go soon so I put the star back where it belongs. I place my feet on the cold floor, swing my bag over my shoulders and step out of the stall. Luckily I don't wear makeup because my face would be a mess otherwise. My eyes are all bloodshot so I turn the tap on and splash cold water on my face trying to freshen myself up. I drag the scrunchie out of my hair so I can readjust it, pulling it back up into a ponytail and fastening it. Inspecting myself in the mirror, I look as normal as I can get. No one will notice anyway. No one ever does. The ringing of the bell has me leaving the bathroom in search of the cafeteria to meet my friends.

Arriving at the chaotic cafeteria, I line up to fill a tray with food which will mostly go uneaten. I locate my usual table and see Blake and Parker are already there. He didn't apologise for getting wasted on Saturday when he was supposed to be driving. All he did was text on Sunday to ask if I got home alright. I guess it's more than the girls did. I didn't hear from them until English today. I couldn't be bothered listening to them talk about Maddox anymore. Apparently he had taken them to another party so I'd ignored them and looked out the window instead. I guess I can't blame them, they probably thought I was fine with Blake and Parker. It would be nice to be considered when they make decisions. I'm growing apart from the girls. We don't have much in common anymore and their drama is so trivial to me now.

As I'm lost in my thoughts, I shuffle forward in line collecting a sandwich today instead of my usual salad. I grab an apple as well in case hunger strikes though it rarely does these days.

Carrying my tray to our table, I catch a glimpse of a familiar blond head exiting through the side door to the benches outside. Following behind him are Rafe and Scott. It must be where they eat their lunch as most of the students have a favoured spot they keep. I take my seat next to Blake as Chloe and Leyla join the table. They all start talking about the party on Saturday and what happened.

"You girls missed Snotty Scotty spewing his guts out after you left," Parker tells us, chuckling.

"Ewww, gross," Chloe says, with her nose scrunched up like she got a whiff of something disgusting.

"Where'd you get to Tam? We didn't see you before we left," Leyla asks. I have to think quickly before replying.

"Oh, I was in the house chatting to one of the girls from my human bio class," I lie, and then quickly take a bite of my sandwich hoping my full mouth will conclude the questioning of my whereabouts. They all accept my lie and continue on with their break down of events.

Leaning in close like she's about to tell a secret, Leyla lowers her voice and says, "You know Elijah said he caught an eye full of some couple going at it on a pool chair while he was playing volleyball." The bit of tasteless sandwich gets lodged in my throat making it hard to swallow all of a sudden.

Chloe screeches, "OMG does he know who it was?" I hold my

breath for the answer, because I know me and Tate were the only ones on the pool chairs, for the majority of the night.

"No, he said all he could make out was the back of the guy's head and the fact he'd angled himself to hide the girl. She was probably giving him a hand job," Leyla says, with a laugh and the others all join in while I force the food down my throat and hope I'm not turning bright red.

"Something crazy always happens at Penny's parties. Remember the time Josh got so drunk and put his hand into the bonfire and they had to call an ambulance?" Chloe chirps in. This leads to them all reminiscing about past events and adding stories they remember. It gives me a minute to think back to my little freak out in human bio and I realise Tate was holding my hand and he was still taking notes. If I revise the theory for today, it will help better prepare me for tomorrow and I won't be a mess like I was today. I see this as a way to escape.

When there's a break in their chatter I say, "Guys I'm gonna get some notes I missed from human bio before next period. I'll catch up with you later." I kiss Blake on the cheek, pick up my bag and take my apple with me leaving my half eaten sandwich and their liveliness behind me. I don't know if I left them because of my notes or the desperate need I have to see the boy I now crave. Either way, it has me pushing open the side door and stepping out into the sunshine in search of him.

_______________________Tate_______________________

Sitting outside eating our lunch, my thoughts wander to Tamsyn like they always do lately. I'm worried about her. I don't know what it was about the eyeballs in class but they freaked her out. I'm glad she let me be there for her too. Holding her hand again felt amazing. I honestly didn't think I would get to hold it again, well not anytime soon. Does this mean Saturday night has changed things between us? I can hope.

"Hello, earth to Tate. Come in, Tate. Are you still with us?" Scott's mocking tone has me looking at him, while JP and Rafe cackle opposite us.

I give Scott a playful shove saying, "Shut up, man."

Laughing back he replies, "You're always away with the fairies these days man. We've all noticed it. And we all know the reason why." Looking at each of them, they all give me their knowing smiles.

"Yeah, yeah whatever guys," I reply, but they laugh at me thinking my daydreaming is funny. Rafe's phone pings and he opens the text smiling at his phone.

"Who has got you smiling?"JP asks him.

"This hottie from the party," he replies, looking up at us with a cheeky grin.

"Bro, not the one I pulled you away from who has a boyfriend, I hope," JP questions.

"Nah dude, it's this other chick I met before her, when I was lining up to use the bathroom," he explains, getting back to his phone.

I take the cap off my water and while taking a swig, Rafe puts his phone down and pipes up with, "You know Elijah is spreading a story about a couple getting wild on the pool chairs at Penny's party," and the water comes flying out of my mouth before I can hold it in. "Umm dude, what the hell?" Rafe grumpily says, wiping his now wet face.

"Sorry man, you caught me off guard," I tell him.

"Why would you be caught off guard?" And I see the exact moment his brain connects the dots because he gets a twinkle in his eye and a big smug grin on his face. "You sly dog. It was you, wasn't it?" he accuses. Scott turns to look at me, gauging my reaction and JP lowers his head shaking it.

"No it wasn't, I was in the house most of the night," I defend. "I'm shocked someone got crazy at the party. I didn't believe you when you said they got out of control." He looks at me a second longer, trying to read my face and while he's watching me his eyes move over my shoulder to something that caught his attention. Then my ears hear the sweetest sound.

"Tate?" Tamsyn quietly says behind me, so I turn around so I can see her. Her eyes are bloodshot like she's been crying. It's all the motivation I need. I'm instantly on my feet reaching for her. Grabbing her arm gently because I don't think she'd appreciate me picking her up and carrying her away like a caveman.

I gaze into her eyes and ask, "Did something happen?" She shakes her head.

"No, no, nothing like that. I didn't get to take notes in human bio so I wondered if I could borrow yours so I'm more prepared for tomorrow," she gives me a half-truth, because I can see through her facade. I know she's been crying. She must have been more upset than she let on this morning.

Turning my back to the guys to try and hide her expression, I ask quietly, "Are you sure there's nothing else bothering you?" Her eyes bore into my soul like she's trying to tell me without using words.

She says, "It doesn't matter." My heart aches for her. What in the world has made this girl think her feelings don't matter? Whenever I try to delve deeper with her I get the same response, 'It doesn't matter.' My blood begins to boil thinking about anyone making her feel unimportant. I clench my jaw trying to contain it.

"It does matter. You matter. You matter to me," I firmly tell her, hoping she hears the sincerity in my voice. Her lower lip trembles. I didn't want to upset her so I run my hand down her arm to her hand, giving it a gentle squeeze to let her know I'm here for her. A small smile creeps onto her face letting me know she isn't going to cry at this moment so I drop my hand to my side and regret it instantly. I'm addicted to her touch already but she's not mine and I don't want people talking about us and causing trouble when nothing is going on. This rumour about the pool chairs is bad enough. Hopefully no one recognised us.

Staring at each other she breaks our bubble by saying, "So can I borrow your notes?"

"Yeah you can take mine for the night; I will copy Scott's in my next class," I tell her.

She gazes at me with a worried expression and says, "Are you sure Scott won't mind?"

With no hesitation I yell over my shoulder to him, "Hey Scott, can I copy your human bio notes next period so Tamsyn can take mine please?"

He doesn't second guess it, replying instantly, "Sure thing man."

"See, no problem at all," I quietly say to her. I'm mentally restraining myself from grabbing her hand in mine.

"Thanks Tate," she quietly says.

"Come, I'll give them to you now," I say, as I step back to the table. I gesture at the guys and say "You guys know Tamsyn? And Tamsyn, you know the guys don't you?"

She timidly lifts her hand and says, "Hi," looking at each of them in turn.

Surprisingly they all smile at her and say, "Hi," back as I'm digging in my bag for my notes.

Rafe cheerily says to her, "Tamsyn, I see an apple in your hand, do you want to join us and finish it?" She inspects her hand with a furrowed brow like she forgot she was holding it. Her eyes connect with mine and she bites her bottom lip unsure whether to sit with us or not. "Take a seat Tamsyn, we won't bite," Rafe playfully encourages her. I nod, conveying it's fine to sit with us. Scott shuffles over to make room for her between us. I locate my book, pull it out and sit down. She swings her legs over the seat, tucks her skirt underneath her and sits down too.

"See, it's exactly like human bio class," Scott jokes, breaking the ice and we all laugh. Tamsyn joins in and I notice this time, it reaches her eyes. Peering up at me, she smiles wide and takes a bite of her apple. Her smile remains on her face as she chews. The boys fall back into their friendly banter and although Tamsyn doesn't say much, the permanent smile on her face says it all. All too soon, the bell for the next period is ringing and we go our separate ways. I hand my book to her before I forget, and watch as she hugs it tightly to her chest, walking away.

Tamsyn

That night I lie face down on the floor with my school books surrounding me, kicking my legs in the air behind me. I pick a random playlist Spotify generated for me and music fills the air. I've been stuck in this fog for so long. Nothing mattered. I was going through the motions trying to survive each day. But today, today was different.

It started off horrible and bawling my eyes out in the bathroom can't be classed as good but from lunchtime onwards, I felt so much lighter. It was all thanks to Tate, and hanging out with his friends at lunch. They are the polar opposite to my friends. They don't thrive on gossip or putting people down. They like each other and enjoy each other's company. It makes me a tad upset, I'm in my final year of high school and I don't have a good group of friends like they do. I've wasted my school years with people who could care less if I'm there or not. With Blake, there's something missing. It might have been good before my dad died but since then my relationship with him has fizzled out. I don't know why he's still with me. We hardly see each other outside of school, we don't talk on the phone anymore and we barely text. And the only time we are the least bit affectionate is when we are saying goodbye which at this stage is a formality more than actual romantic feelings. I don't think it's a good sign, especially when I've been more touchy-feely with Tate than my own boyfriend in the last few days.

Don't Think. Just Breathe.

Tate. Thinking of him makes me remember his human bio notebook. I pull his book towards me and flick my thumb over the pages. There's a page in the back with a piece ripped out of it. The shape of the hole is familiar for some reason. I keep flicking through his pages and there's another ripped out page. My brain clicks and I think of the notes he's given me. I push myself up off the ground and take a couple of steps to my bedside table to retrieve his notes I keep there. I pull them both out, having already placed the star back there after school to keep it safe. I sit down on the carpet and cross my legs finding the ripped pages. First is the page that was ripped out. I get the note with 'You are enough' on it and line it up. It fits perfectly. Excited for what is to come, I flick the pages to the one I need and place my star in its spot. It's a bit worn around the edges from all the times I've held it but otherwise it fits exactly in the space. So it's this book, his notes come from. Having it with me makes me more connected to him in a way. Wanting to do something special for him like he does for me, I try to think of a note I could leave him but nothing comes to mind. All I want to gain from it is a smile. With that in mind, I flip to the inside back cover and in the bottom right corner I draw a smiley face. Not too big though, I don't want it to be obvious. Hopefully he will come across it one day randomly. Fingers crossed he makes the connection and realises it's from me. On second thought, being brave I flip to the next blank page after his notes on eye dissection. Right at the top, so he won't miss it, I write my name and number. This way he can use it if he wants to which I'm sure he will. And if he doesn't, I can pretend like he hasn't seen it. It will take the sting out of his rejection.

With that done, I get back to my homework. I find the notes that I need and begin copying them into my own book. I admire his handwriting because for a guy his writing is pretty and a bit dainty. I giggle to myself because I wouldn't have expected that of him. He's written on the notes I've received but there wasn't enough written to get the full scope of his penmanship. With a smile on my face I get lost in the work, copying it word for word. I will have to read over it before bed so that I'm prepared for tomorrow. I hope I can hold it together long enough to get through the class. I finish copying what I need then pack all my books up in my bag so they're ready to go in the morning. I put my precious notes from Tate back in their safe place beside my bed. With the main light on, I get into bed with Tate's book to read over the dissection notes. While reading and rereading his work, my eyes get droopy and I fall into a soundless sleep with his book clutched to my chest.

My alarm music stirs me from my slumber. The light is off but I'm sure I fell asleep with it on. Mum must have come in and turned it off for me. No dreams tormenting me last night. It's the first night in a long time I've had a dreamless sleep and woken up feeling refreshed. I spring out of bed ready to take on the day, hoping human bio won't affect me too negatively. With my new found positive attitude, I get ready for school hoping it will carry me through human bio without any major freak outs. I'm a girl. It should entitle me to at least one minor freak out when dealing with gross slimy eyeballs.

_______________________________Tate_________________________________

After the events at lunch yesterday, I thought JP and the guys might give me the third degree about Tamsyn but they didn't mention her at all. Maybe they're coming around to the fact she isn't as vile as they thought she was. It surprised the shit out of me too when she rocked up to our bench yesterday. I wonder if she can feel the pull, an invisible force at work drawing us both together.

"You think Tamsyn will grace us with her presence at lunch again?" JP cuts through my inner thoughts, as I space out on our way to school.

"Umm…. I don't know man. She had a reason to come over yesterday," I say to him. He stares at me as he pulls up to a stop sign.

"And you aren't reason enough?" he asks, with a crinkling around his eyes and a tug of his lips.

"Like you said, she's with Blake. And I think we could both use each other as a friend more than anything else right now," I tell him, while leering out the window. I don't want to delve deeper into it right now. He must know not to go there so turns up the car radio to fill the silence so we don't have to talk any more. This suits me fine.

When he parks the car at school, I see Rafe and Scott greeting each other not too far ahead so I call out to them. An idea is brewing in my mind.

"Hey guys, I have a favour to ask. Do you think you could lend me a hand in human bio today?" I say to them, as I get closer.

"Yeah dude, what's up?" Rafe says, as Scott says

"Sure." I have great friends who give their help willingly, without knowing what it is first. I fill them in on yesterday's events.

"So you probably didn't notice, but Tamsyn was having a bit of a freak out yesterday because of the dissection.

"Ah is this why she was fidgety when class first started?" Scott's observing nature showing.

"Yeah something to do with the eyeballs made her agitated. I'm not entirely sure what it was about. We are doing the actual dissection today so I thought we could work closely with her and try keep the atmosphere upbeat. Hopefully it will keep her distracted and her thoughts off whatever triggered her yesterday," I fill them in on my plan. "You guys in?" I ask, unsure if they'll agree.

"Yeah no worries," Rafe says.

"You think she will freak out today?" Scott wants to know.

"I don't know man, she was bad yesterday, but I managed to keep her calm. I'm hoping we can do the same today," I say with worry in my voice.

"We've got her dude, don't you worry at all," Rafe tells me.

"Thanks guys," I say to them, as Rafe throws his arm over my shoulder and we walk towards the wide stone steps at the school entrance. As if my body can sense her presence, I glimpse to the right.

There she is, right by the last row of cars before we start climbing the steps. What I see takes my breath away. She's smiling and I instantly know it's a real smile because this smile meets her eyes. The problem is, it's not directed at me, it's directed at Blake; her boyfriend. I quickly turn my head so she doesn't see me and my heart cracks. Silly, I know. She has a boyfriend yet I still hoped she felt the same connection I did. Friends, it's all I'm supposed to be aiming for. Yet my head is having trouble convincing my heart it's all I want.

With today being Tuesday, we don't have human bio until right before lunch so me and the guys' part ways with our 'distract Tamsyn' plan ready for action. The positive mood I'd started the day with has been extinguished and I find myself distracted during class.

The image of Tamsyn grinning at Blake is like a spear to my gut and I can't shake the unwanted feelings it brings with it. I'm in Calculus class first this morning and we are working on equations from our textbooks so I can take my time, letting my self-loathing simmer in my mind. I persevere and try to push it aside, choosing to focus on my work. I've been so distracted in my thoughts of Tamsyn lately, I've ignored my own issues buried inside. What a hypocrite I am. I have been chomping at the bit to know all her secrets and the cause of her pain but not dealing with or sharing my own guilt and shame.

The longer I sit here, the more infuriated I become. I start to crack so I hastily shove my books in my bag. The banging noises I'm making have heads turning my way but I could care less, I need to get out of here.

Bag in hand, half jogging to the door, I hear my maths teacher Mr. Finnegan yell, "Tate, where are you going?" I don't give him a second thought as I'm past the point of stopping. Slamming the door as I exit, I race down the hall, exiting into the fresh air and running wherever my feet take me.

By the time I'm out of breath, I drop my bag on the grass and place my hands on my head, trying to draw air into my lungs. They're screaming for oxygen, as my mind screams for silence. My skin is tingling from the rage boiling below the surface. I can't get enough breath into my lungs. My breaths are coming too fast and too short. A panic attack; it's the last thing I need right now. I haven't had a full blown one since I've arrived in this town. I thought leaving home I had left the anxiety that caused the panic attacks behind but I guess it's not the case. My heart is going to burst out of my chest any second. I need to get control of this. I slump to the ground and lean against the goal post. I've run all the way out to the football field.

I think back to Dr Lawson's advice on how to recover after a panic attack. I close my eyes, drawing a slow breath into my lungs and I focus on the rhythm. In and out. In and out. My heart rate slows as I exhale longer, finally getting my breathing under control. Don't think. Don't think. Don't think! I push all my thoughts to the side where I can keep them contained.

I hear the faint bell sounds for the next period. I'm still trying to recover and catch my breath; I'm in no state to go to class. I know I shouldn't be alone. I search my pocket for my phone and send JP a message. Not five minutes have passed and I can see him sprinting my way from a distance.

"Bro, what's wrong?" his distress has his voice shaking. Widened eyes lined with worry stare at me. "What are you doing out here?" he questions.

"Panic attack," is all I say, and I see the pity take over. I continue to focus on my breathing. JP can't help how he feels right now. People who don't understand my panic attacks always get the same expression of pity on their face. I used to lash out when I'd see their concern change to pity but it's happened so many times now I've become immune to their response.

JP drops his butt to the grass beside me and catches his own breath. We sit for a good ten minutes, in our own thoughts, focussed on our breathing. Since I moved here I've noticed one thing about JP. He isn't good with silence.

Chapter 8

Before long he's asking, "Do you want to talk about it?" I stare out at the length of the field facing the school feeling like it's miles away.

I reply, "I couldn't control my thoughts today. They rushed up on me and I had to get away before I snapped at someone. I ran out in the middle of my Calculus class."

"Oh bro. And this is the first time it's happened here?" he asks, and something about his voice makes me think he knows more about my panic attacks than he's letting on.

"Did my mum say something to you?" I ask him, with an arched brow.

He chuckles saying, "You know our mums talk non-stop. Yours told mine about the panic attacks and my mum told me. Don't be mad, bro. They're worried. We all are," I nod my head. I don't want them all worrying about me. "You sure something didn't set you off?" he asks like he knows there is but doesn't want to say it outright. I don't want him blaming Tamsyn for triggering me when she did nothing wrong. All she did was have a genuine smile on her face and I flipped a gasket. No, I'll keep this information to myself.

"Nah man, I reached boiling point this morning and couldn't contain it any longer."

He accepts my response for truth and asks, "Are you going to be all good for next period?" He looks at his watch, "It's going to start in ten minutes. I've got to hand in my history assignment so I've got to go." Next period; I search my brain for my schedule and it's human bio next. Thoughts of helping Tamsyn through the class override everything else I'm feeling and I'm on my feet before I answer JP.

"Yeah man, I'm good. Let's head back," I tell him, throwing my bag over my shoulder. I stretch out my hand to help pull him up to his feet. We walk in silence back to school, fist bumping before we veer off in different directions.

Chapter 9

_____________________ Tamsyn _____________________

The longer English class drags on, the sweatier my hands become. Tate hasn't arrived. He mustn't be at school today so I guess this means I'll be on my own for our eye dissection. The thought alone is causing me to panic. I notice Scott staring at the door; I wonder if he's hoping Tate will walk in too. It's nearly the end of the period and he still hasn't arrived. I hope he isn't sick. Let's hope he sees my number in his book when I give it back to him. It would make contacting him a lot easier and save me from all this stress of not knowing.

The bell rings signalling the end of class so Mr. Barnes dismisses us and we start packing up. I take my time, not in a rush to get to human bio now. Not now, because Tate won't be there to help me through it. Leyla and Chloe wave goodbye as they leave. The class is empty now so I've got no excuse to stay. I drag my feet down the hall, dread filling me with every step. I wipe my sweaty palms on my skirt trying to dry them but my apprehension makes them sweat more. I turn the handle on the door fearing how the next hour is going to go. I enter, shuffling my way to my desk with my head down.

Ms. Chadwick's voice brings me out of my funk, "Okay class, let's get straight into it today. We will be working in pairs from our tables." I gulp as it's now confirmed I'll be by myself. "Can one person from each group come up and retrieve their eyeball specimen and tools you are going to need. No funny business either kids. Rafe, I'm looking at you," I hear her warn. I'm nearly at my desk, head still down. I close my eyes and take a deep inhale preparing myself for what's about to come.

Surprisingly I'm blessed with the familiar earthy scent I know belongs to Tate. Simultaneously, my eyes snap open as I feel his touch on my hand as he tugs me towards him. He's twisted in his chair so he moves me between his spread legs as if it's normal for us to be this close. We stare at each other as he holds my hand, running his thumb back and forth in a calming gesture. My heart sighs with relief because he's here.

"You're here," I tenderly say, with a genuine smile on my face.

"Of course I am. I told you I would be." He returns my smile with one of his own but his eyes are tense like something is wrong. He wasn't in English either which has me concerned.

"Is everything alright with you? You weren't in English," I say, and without thinking I lift my hand and wipe my thumb across his forehead like I can erase the stress lining his face. He audibly sighs and brings me back to reality. I drop his hand and inch back from him.

With an amused expression on his face he says, "Everything is fine now. Nothing a dose of you won't fix." He winks at me. My face heats up and a smile tugs at my lips. I turn away and pull my book out of my bag along with Tate's book.

"Thanks for the notes. You're a lifesaver," I say, returning his book to him.

"You're welcome. Now do you want me to get our eyeball so we are good to go?" he asks, and then must see the hesitation on my face. "It's going to be alright. I'm here, Sweetness," he whispers, using his secret name for me which makes my heart sing, sending a relaxing calm through me.

"Can you try not to get a blue eye, please?" I quietly ask him.

He nods saying, "No problem," as he bounces off his seat towards the front of the class. I push my chair to the side so I can stand at the desk like most of the class. He returns with a tray carrying a blue cow's eye, a scalpel, scissors, wax paper and paper towels, setting it down on our desk. On the board, there's a diagram of the cow's eye to use for direction.

"Sorry, they only had a blue one left," Tate apologises.

"Right class. Let's get started. Starting off we are going to examine the eye and I want you to see how many features you can identify. And yes, it will be easier if you handle the eye. Please remember to wash your hands at the end of class. Let's start. I'll be walking around the class calling out further instructions too so keep up," Ms. Chadwick instructs us on how to proceed. Inspecting the eyeball closely, my hands shake. Tate, perceptive as always, sees my panic set in. Most of the class is preoccupied, excited about the gross prospect of playing with their eyeballs so they don't notice us for which I'm thankful. The last thing I need is the school rumour mill talking about me. Tate sits back in his chair with his legs spread. He snakes a hand around my waist pulling my back towards his chest.

I find myself naturally sitting in his lap a bit and he rests his chin on my shoulder whispering to me, "Breathe, Sweetness. We're going to get through this." I relax into his touch and he brings the other arm around me to squeeze me tighter. In the back of my subconscious, I know I shouldn't be this close to him but I can't remember the reason why when it's so right. "Now tell me what exactly about the eyeball is freaking you out?" he gently probes. His touch has fried all my sensors so I don't even think when I tell him the truth

"My dad's eyes were blue and I got a flash of the day I found him on the kitchen floor. The day he died." I timidly confess to him. He holds me even tighter like he's pressing my broken pieces back together. I wish it were this simple. My lips shake with the pain my confession has brought to the surface.

He must notice something change in me because he eases me with,

"Sshh, sshh, sshh." His grip loosens and he uses his hands to turn me around to face him resting his hands on my hips. I see concern on his face. He looks at me with such emotion, I can see him trying to take all my pain away so I never have to hurt again. If he could, it would be a miracle.

Without taking his eyes off of mine, he calls over my shoulder to Scott, "Scott, can we switch eyeballs please?" I don't hear a response but Tate's hand leaves my hip. Out of the corner of my eye, I see a disgusting brown eyeball roll towards his open palm on the table ready to catch it.

I can't help my mortified reaction, "Ewww Scott, that's gross," I say, turning out of Tate's grip trying to suppress my giggling.

"It was Rafe," Scott defends, pointing his thumb over his shoulder at a cheeky grinned Rafe who shrugs. Tate places the brown eye in the tray and picks up the blue one.

"Think Fast," he yells, while tossing it into the air by the boys.

Luckily Rafe catches it with little effort saying, "Touchdown! The crowd goes wild," waving the eyeball around in the air. His comedic act has us all in hysterics letting Ms. Chadwick know we are up to no good.

"Boys down the back, please behave," she yells. We all chortle behind our hands trying to get back to the task at hand.

"So do you want to touch it?" Tate asks, and I scrunch my face up at the thought. He tries not to laugh at me, "I'll take that as a no," and grabs the eyeball. He stands up and side by side, we examine the disgusting specimen. We are able to identify the sclera, the fat and muscle and the cornea. Next, Ms. Chadwick directs us to cut the fat and muscle away. Tate picks up the scissors and cuts away at the pink and white fleshy meat.

"Make sure you both take turns," Ms. Chadwick's voice rings through the classroom. Great, I'm going to have to touch the thing.

"When you've cut all the fat away, you are going to get the scalpel and make an incision in the cornea until a clear liquid is released. This is the aqueous humour. Please be careful. The scalpels are sharp."

"It's not that bad, Tamsyn," Tate says, to me as he holds his hand out to pass me the eye. I take it and nearly drop it.

"Ewww it's slimy," I say, which has him laughing.

"Here, I'll help you," he offers, and hands me the scalpel so I can take it safely. "You want to cut this part here," he says, as he points, giving me direction. I carefully push the scalpel into the slimy flesh and I'm horrified when the liquid escapes running down my fingers.

"Ugh, this is so gross," I say, while Tate is trying not to laugh at me. "Glad you find me funny," I say trying not to laugh back at him.

"Next, use the scalpel to make a small incision through the sclera in the middle of the eye then finish cutting with your scissors. You will end up with two halves if you've done it correctly," Ms. Chadwick instructs.

"Since you've got the scalpel, you might as well make the incision. I'll use the scissors," Tate suggests, so I cut a slice on the side of the eye, place the scalpel on the tray and hand the eye back to Tate. Our fingers lightly touch sending a shockwave through my hand. Our eyes connect and he grins. Did he feel it too? Tate gets to work cutting around the eye and now we have two pieces with the cornea on one side.

"Class, I do hope you are keeping up. You should have the cornea separated by now. I want you to place it on your tray. Then you are going to cut and listen to the sound it makes," Ms. Chadwick says, issuing our next instructions.

"You can do the honours," Tate tells me, as he points to the cornea part.

"You're so kind," I tell him sarcastically. I'm glad he finds my repulsion funny. I pick up the scalpel and cut through the thick cornea which makes a crunching side as it breaks. Gross. I never would have thought cow eyes could be this disturbing. I can hear Rafe and Scott cracking jokes behind me with their eyeball. They must find it as funny as Tate does. Ms. Chadwick fires out more instructions. Tate and I work together, him helping me when he sees I'm unsure. I think he's highly amused at how repulsed I am.

"Class, the bell is about to go but we are going to work through. I will excuse you from your following period after lunch so you can eat then," Ms. Chadwick says, as the bell rings. No one was in a hurry to leave anyway, all too entranced with what we are doing.

Working well together, we manage to get the lens out which I find fascinating. You can hold the lens up to words and see them through it. This dissection thing isn't as bad as I thought. Don't get me wrong, it's pretty gross but in an enthralling way. As the class continues, we find the retina and the optic nerve. Ms. Chadwick informs us the blind spot is where the retina attaches to the back of the eye. My favourite part is when she explains the Tapetum. It's a colourful, shiny material which is found behind the retina. It reflects light. It was a pretty end to all the gruesomeness. Without realising how much time has passed, the bell is ringing again for the end of lunch.

I smile at Tate and say, "Thank you, you made class way more bearable." He shyly smiles at me back.

"Okay class, I want you to wrap all the eyeball material up into paper towels then put them in the rubbish bags coming around. Make sure you don't forget to wash your hands thoroughly before you leave, especially since you are going to be eating straight after this. You can make your way to the cafeteria and eat quietly there for the next period," Ms. Chadwick tells us. Tate gathers up all the bits of our cow eye and wraps it up, disposing of it in the plastic bag.

"Man, that was so much fun," I hear Rafe say to Scott, and I can't help but giggle. He's such a child sometimes. We all line up at the sinks taking turns, washing the filthy substance from our hands.

As I'm collecting my bag, Tate asks, with an edge of uncertainty in his voice, "So do you want to eat lunch with us?"

"Of course," I reply, with a big smile on my face as it's a no brainer. I don't want our time together to end yet.

Don't Think. Just Breathe.

Chapter 10

Tate

Our whole class shuffles quietly through the empty halls, headed to the cafeteria. I walk freely beside Tamsyn and it feels so right, with her next to me. I don't usually see her outside of classes. Yesterday was the exception. I wonder if she would seek me out for no other reason than to hang out. I don't know. As we all lined up to get our food trays, I let Tamsyn go in front of me. When I see her about to walk away with a sandwich and an apple on her plate, I hook my finger in the collar of her shirt and pull her gently back towards me. She gawks at me, wondering what the hell I'm doing.

"This can't be all you're going to eat?" I ask, examining her measly tray of food.

She follows my eyes to her tray and responds with, "I'm not a big eater." She tries to justify her choices but I'm not buying it.

"Here, add this," I say, as I grab a punnet of grapes. On second thought, "Oh and this too," I add, handing her a double chocolate chip muffin because all girls love chocolate right? She looks at me as if I'm insane for giving her more food but I could care less, she needs to eat. She's too skinny. As she's contemplating on how she will eat it all, I pile my tray up with sandwiches, pizza, fries, oranges, a muffin and an apple. Being a growing boy, I never get full. Rafe and Scott behind me are doing exactly the same thing. When my tray is full, I lead the way to a table by the window. If we can't be outside, we might as well get some sun shining on us while we eat. Tamsyn sits down and I take a seat next to her wanting to be as close to her as I can.

Before I start digging into my food, I ask her, "How did you find the dissection? I noticed you weren't as anxious as you were yesterday."

She angles her body to face me, taking my hand in both of hers and with a twinkle in her eye she says, "I wouldn't have gotten through class without you. I'm truly grateful." She's staring at me with big, bright eyes and I can tell she is being genuine.

"It was nothing. I would have done the same for any of my friends," I tell her truthfully.

"Hmmm, I think we are going to be the best of friends," she says, with a huge smile on her face. She drops my hand, turns back to her food and grabs the muffin. Rafe and Scott sit down a moment later and it proves my suspicions. It was their presence making her pull away from me. Maybe she doesn't want them to see how affectionate we've become. It might be weird if they saw us being intimate with each other when she has a boyfriend.

The guys being guys, start bringing up gross details about the eyeball and how the fluid squirted from their one when Scott cut it. I'm sure it's for Tamsyn's benefit and they have her giggling the whole time. She's so busy laughing and enjoying herself; I don't think she realises she ate her whole muffin, apple, sandwich and half of her grapes. I think it's the most food I've ever seen her consume since I've known her. It's nice to see this side of her. Eating and laughing instead of being closed off and distant. I smile to myself, hoping I'm the reason behind her new found smiles.

"Tate, how come you didn't make it to English?" Scott throws me off with his question. With the dissection taking so long, I had forgotten about my previous melt down.

"Something came up I needed to take care of," I lie, but I hope it sounds convincing. I see Tamsyn peer up at me. I wasn't convincing enough. I get the feeling she doubts me. Luckily, Scott isn't bothered by my answer so the topic gets dropped which I'm thankful for. I don't want pity from them, especially Tamsyn, if I have to explain my panic attacks.

Vibrations coming from my pocket have me tugging my phone out and staring at the screen. I stare at the caller display but choose not to answer, letting the call go to voicemail instead.

Three sets of eyes stare at me and Rafe dares to ask, "Aren't you going to answer?"

"Nah, it's just my dad," I casually answer, putting my phone away and continue eating my food. All of a sudden, there's an eerie silence so I glance up from my tray and watch the guys and their expressions. Their concerned eyes are focussed on the girl beside me. Turning her way, I shatter. The broken girl I met that first night has appeared. Her head is down, her shoulders are folding in on themselves as if she can make herself so small we won't notice she's there. I'm clueless as to what caused her change in mood so suddenly.

"Tamsyn?" I ask cautiously, but she doesn't move. She's too far gone in her mind, she can't hear me. With a screech, I push my chair back and kneel before her, turning her chair my way. I turn to the guys for help but they sit there unmoving not knowing what to do. I grasp her tiny hands in mine, they are shaking. I try to catch her eye but I can't so I grab her chin between my finger and thumb and lift her eyes up. Pools of tears sit contained on her eyelids, waiting to fall. Her eyes are aimed at me but they are vacant. Her spirit has deserted her body, not being able to handle the emotion she's feeling. My broken girl is making me break right along with her. I will keep trying until I succeed.

"Tamsyn?" I whisper softly, trying to draw her back to me but it still doesn't work. My worry for Tamsyn overrides what the guys might think if they hear me. "Sweetness?" I say, hoping my name for her will get through the barricade keeping me out. It works! Her eyes show some life behind them once again but the stream of tears start falling down her face. "Tell me what's wrong please?" I ask, pleading with her.

She answers, whimpering, "Your dad," but I don't understand.

"Are you upset I didn't answer my dad's call?" I ask her, still a bit confused.

That one line out of my mouth takes her away from me and a rage I've never seen on her before unleashes, "Don't you know I'd give anything to get a call from my dad?" The air from my lungs whooshing out of me as I connect the dots too late. "You sat there and ignored him like he didn't matter. Who cares what he was going to say. He's worried about you because it's what good fathers do. And he must be a good father to have raised someone like you. But you took him for granted. He won't be around forever and you'll regret it when he's gone." She's huffing now, out of breath from her speech but I can see the fire in her eyes.

"Sweetness, please," I don't know what to say right now.

"I'm gonna go," she tells me, grabbing her things and before I can plead with her to stay, she's gone. I stay on my knees, completely lost until a hand on my shoulder brings me back to the present. She's right, I deserved it.

"Come on dude, up you get," Rafe says, as he sticks out a hand to help me. Accepting his help, I drop into my chair. Blurry vision has me blinking and water splatters my face. What the hell? I swipe at my face and the realisation hits me; I'm crying. I chance a glance at the guys and their wide eyed stares bore into me. I see Rafe pulling his phone from his pocket probably texting JP, alerting him something is wrong. My breathing speeds up and I know a panic attack isn't far off. I hate how out of control they make me feel. I do the one thing I can think of. I grab my bag and run. This time my feet don't stop until I get home, locking myself in my room and letting the uninvited tears wash away my pain.

_________________________ **Tamsyn** _________________________

My whole body is shaking and the volcano has erupted. I'm going to the one place I feel safe at this school...my sanctuary. It's empty as most students are still in class so I lock myself in my favoured stall. Dropping the seat, I climb up holding myself together because this time I broke myself. I didn't mean to take my feelings out on Tate. He didn't deserve it. And I did it in front of his friends too. Oh my gosh! What do they think of me now? I can't believe I did that. My breaking heart physically pains me enough, I rub my chest to soothe it. I wish I could fade away right now. Jealousy seeps through my veins. All because of a simple phone call. Tate has a dad who's alive to receive calls from and he ignored him. It's not fair. I want my dad back. Why did he have to die?

I sit in the stall until the end of school. Girls come in and out not thinking anything of the occupied stall at the end and who could be hiding inside. I should leave but my feet won't move. I still clutch my legs to me, as if I can hold myself together from falling apart permanently. The door swinging open draws my attention to it because two familiar voices follow. It's Leyla and Chloe. I can tell they're standing in front of the mirror checking their makeup because neither one went into a stall.

"So is Blake coming around tonight?" Chloe asks intrigued. Blake. Why are they talking about Blake?

"Yeah, he's been around every night this week," Leyla excitedly tells her. I'm confused but I stay as quiet as I can to continue eavesdropping.

"Did he say if he's going to break up with her yet?" Chloe asks, and the air leaves my lungs. Blake and Leyla are together? Behind my back?

"Yeah, he said he's waiting for the right time. He still feels sorry for her because of her dad dying. Like I care; I want them broken up so I can proudly say he's mine. It's been long enough. It will be our three month anniversary next week, you know?" she smugly tells Chloe.

"OMG that is soooo cute," I hear Chloe say enthusiastically. They exit the bathroom leaving me behind in a state of shock at their sudden revelation. I knew they were bitches but I never thought it was directed at me. And Blake. He's been with her for three months?? Why not break up with me instead of dragging this out? Utterly betrayed and alone. Why am I always alone? I have no one.

I need to get out of here and get home. I'm not going with Blake. I would rather walk than get in a car with him right now. The coast is clear so I release the hold on my legs. They're all stiff from being cramped up for so long. I exit the stall and quickly assess my appearance in the mirror. I know I look like utter shit but I couldn't care less right now. I want to get home. I'll be safe at home. I keep my head down as I exit the bathroom and try to pass unseen through the school corridors. Unfortunately I have to go out to the car park to get to the front gate. As I'm making my escape, I hear my name called in the not so friendly voice I remember from the other night. Shit, not now. I don't need this now.

"Tamsyn!" he yells louder, the closer he gets. Before I can make a run for it, he grabs my shirt sleeve roughly and halts my escape. He twists me towards him and doesn't mask his anger. It's written all over his face. He's pissed. The car park is still half full, with people taking their time to leave today. "I thought I told you not to hurt him, Tamsyn," his gruff voice makes me tremble.

"I didn't mean to," I explain, while fighting back more tears. JP doesn't care about my tears, he cares about Tate. Here he is fighting for Tate while I'm alone with nobody fighting for me. Why can't he see my struggle? Why can't he see I'm at breaking point? He's pulled an audience now. They can sense his anger towards me and want in on the gossip as to why. "Is he alright?" I try to find out but he chuckles at me.

"What do you think? Of course, he's not alright. He took off and I have no clue where he is. I told you he was vulnerable and to leave him alone. But no, the Ice Queen couldn't help hurt someone else, could she?" He spits his vehemence at me. Past his shoulder I spot Rafe and Scott coming towards us. They try to stop him but they get there too late. His last line breaks me. "I don't know what he sees in you. Stay away from him. I will do whatever I have to, to keep him safe from the likes of you." My world stops for a second, I'm on a downward spiral and there's no coming back for me. My brain takes the lid off the containment and it spews out at JP in a haunting, shrill voice I don't recognise

"You need to keep him safe? What about me? Why doesn't anyone want to keep me safe? Why doesn't anyone see me struggling?" My words take on a life of their own, being directed at everyone in the near vicinity. "I'm right in front of you drowning but you don't see. You don't care. Why won't anyone save me?" My eyes zoom in on JP and my voice lowers as my essence deserts me, leaving nothing in its place. "You can see the pain on my face yet you choose to continue to beat me down and break me. Don't worry. Now I know I'm beyond being saved." With my last ounce of energy I sprint away; away from all my brokenness, away from the loneliness and away from me.

_______________________________Tate_________________________________

I've been in my room since I left school early. I managed to contain my panic attack. I did my breathing exercises. The run home helped too. Letting my tears run until they dried helped make me numb again. I've pushed the reset button on my emotions, where they wait until they fill up and blow over again.

I'm listening to some music when I hear a loud 'BANG, BANG, BANG'. I ignore it knowing it's likely JP, worried about me. I bet Rafe filled him in on what happened at the cafeteria. I don't want to see him and have to explain myself. It was bad enough the guys saw me cry, I don't want to relive it with JP.

'BANG, BANG, BANG' There he goes again. It doesn't sound like he's going to leave me alone. I get off my bed, determined to open the door so he can see my face and then close it again. However when I open it, I'm shocked at what I see. JP stands there with a bloody nose and what appears to be the start of a black eye.

"What the fuck?" I say, then notice Rafe and Scott are behind him.

"We need to talk," is all JP says, as he pushes past me into my room with Rafe and Scott filing in behind him.

"What the hell happened to you?" I ask him, ready to fight whoever did it to him.

"He deserved it," Scott casually says, and my eyes shift to him. I see his knuckles are all bloodied and busted up. My eyes bulge out of my head from shock. What a day to miss school.

"Yeah, I probably did deserve it but we got more important issues bro." The guilt washes over his face and makes me uneasy in the pit of my stomach. I sit back on my bed so I'm better prepared for what they are about to say.

"It's Tamsyn," JP says, as all the air is forced from my lungs.

"What happened?" I manage to croak, my throat suddenly dry. With his head held in shame, he says, "The guys told me what she said to you so I confronted her in the car park after school. I yelled at her."

As my anger builds towards JP, Rafe pipes in with, "He didn't yell at her, he went off his rocker at her. Scott and I tried to get him to calm him down but he was too far gone."

Then Scott adds the kicker, "And it's not the worst part. Tamsyn broke down and started screaming all this tortured stuff at him. She said she was beyond being saved then ran away." With those words, the spear returns to my gut and twists.

Immediately I'm on my feet, "Where is she?" I direct at no one in particular.

"We don't know," they all say in unison, with shame on their faces.

My rage is still simmering so I turn my eyes to JP, glaring at him and say, "If something has happened to her, I'll never forgive you. I told you she reminded me of her. You should have known better. This could have pushed her over the edge." His head sags to his chest letting my words sink in. I am always so helpless when it comes to the women in my life. For once, I need something to go my way.

"Does anyone have her number?" They all peer at each other, shaking their heads. "Damn it," I mutter. "How long has it been since school finished?" I ask, not knowing the time as I've been cocooned in my room.

"It's been a few hours. We tried driving around to find her. But we couldn't. She ran off and we don't know in which direction," Scott tells me.

"Did you check her house?" I ask, trying to get as much information as I can.

"We drove past it but nobody was home. We followed the route we thought she may have taken but didn't come across her," JP says quietly.

"Take me to her house. I'll knock on the door," I tell JP, as I put on my socks and sneakers, determined to find her.

"Okay, let's all go. I'm worried about her too," Scott informs me, and it makes me pause for a second. I scan the room and take in all their expressions. They range from guilt, worry and concern. Maybe they care about her as much as I do.

We all pile into JP's car and he speeds straight to Tamsyn's house, running a few close orange lights on the way. As he parks up right outside her house, we have no plan in place. I want to barge up there and bang down the door but the others don't think it's a good idea. Rafe the charmer is in charge and we all agree to follow his lead. Four big guys walking up to Tamsyn's front door must look weird, but Rafe has a way with everyone so he's sure he can charm Tamsyn's mum if he needs to. He knocks on the door and we wait. Nothing happens.

"Shit, no one is here," Scott says, from behind me.

"Try again," I tell Rafe impatiently. I'm shaking from wanting to know she's alright. Please let her be alright. Rafe knocks again on the door, this time much longer and louder. A few moments pass and we can hear loud hurried footsteps coming to the door. Please be Tamsyn, I beg. The door is wrenched open and a short dishevelled lady with big brown eyes and chocolate brown hair, the same as Tamsyn's, stands there. I focus on the woman before us, she's on the verge of tears.

"Hi Mrs. Winter, I'm Rafe Trenton. You might know my mum, Sharon Trenton, from the school's bake sales through the years." Her eyes lift up to the sound of Rafe's cheery voice and the wheels spin behind her eyes trying to place Sharon.

"Oh yes dear, I remember Sharon, how is she?" she asks.

"She's good ma'am. She always said you made the best peanut brownies at the bake sales," Rafe uses his most charming voice, trying to build a rapport with her.

She chuckles with sadness, saying, "Oh, she's too kind. Now how can I help you gentlemen?"

"We are all good friends of Tamsyn's mam but none of us have her number. We were worried about her so we thought we would pop around to see her," Rafe tells her honestly. I don't think it is a good idea because in this day and age, what good friend wouldn't have her number. Relief washes over her face though, so it must have worked.

"Oh thank goodness, come in," she says, quickly grabbing Rafe's shirt and pulling him through the doorway with us all following.

"What's wrong? " I ask, now we're inside her home. Tamsyn's mum wrings her hands as she paces back and forth.

"You're good friends with her? Do you know where Blake is?" her mum questions.

"Don't worry about Blake right now mam, Tate here is probably closer to Tamsyn now than Blake is," he says, smiling at her then turns to me and sticks his bottom lip out and shrugs, suggesting it's true. Her mum studies me. She's never met me so I don't blame her.

I try to ease her mind by saying, "Do you know Mrs. Peterson? JP's mum?" I say pointing to JP who she recognises instantly. "She's my aunty", and it's all she needs, knowing my aunt is the nicest person around. "You were going to tell us about Tamsyn?" I try to bring her attention back to our main focus.

"Yes, yes. She came home from school with this haunted expression on her face. I tried to call out to her but she wouldn't listen. It's as if she couldn't hear me. She locked herself in her bathroom and all I could hear was her whimpering over the running water. I couldn't get to her. Her door doesn't unlock from my side. I'm worried about her. I was hoping she would come out but she's been in there since she got home from school." My heart is beating out of my chest.

"Take me to her," I demand, and her mum rushes up the stairs with all of us closely behind her. She turns down the hall and indicates to a door on the right.

"She's in there," she says, sounding more worried now. I try to rattle the door handle but it's firmly locked, so I put my ear to the door to listen and I hear running water but nothing else.

"Mrs. Winter, I'm sorry but I'm gonna have to break down your door," I tell her, not caring whether she will try to stop me or not.

"Okay," is all I hear from her small form. She moves off to the side of the hall out of the way and I turn my back on the door. Lifting my leg, I kick backwards and the door flings off its hinges.

We all cram in the doorway and my heart stops. Tamsyn's frail form is hunched in a ball, hugging her legs to her under the running water. She's still in her school uniform, shoes included.

"Grab some towels," I instruct no one in particular, but hear someone scurry off to get some. Seeing the state she's in, I don't know if JP's presence will make it worse so I say, "JP, how about you wait down stairs." Understanding dawns on his face. He gives me a small nod of his head and disappears out the door. I open the shower stall and turn the water off. It's freezing; stuck on the coldest setting. "Shit, it's freezing," I tell the guys as her mum hurries back in the door. I bend down to Tamsyn but her head is hidden from view, tucked into her arms. Her whole body is shivering. "Give me a towel," I say behind me, and I'm handed one. I wrap the fluffy white towel around her. Sliding my hand under her legs I pull her to my chest, standing up. Gosh, she weighs nothing dripping wet. She's tucked herself together so tightly, she's frozen in place. "We need to get her dry," I say, turning to her mum.

"Here, come to her room," she instructs me, and we all file out and follow Tamsyn's mum to another door down the hall. She flings it open and as I walk in, all I smell is Tamsyn. Her scent surrounds me while I hold her broken form in front of me.

Rafe stands there with some more towels so I say, "Help me dry her man." He hands a towel to Scott and both holding towels, they gently help me pat her dry.

"Dude, she's going to have to get those wet clothes off," Rafe tries to whisper at me, as it's awkward in front of her mum. He's right, she'll never get dry like this.

I give him a silent nod to go ahead so he says to her mum, "Mam, she's going to have to get those wet clothes off. If we leave her on the bed, could you change her?" I can hear the concern dripping from his voice. Seeing her in this state has rattled me and all of my friends.

Her mum looks at me and says, "I might need help. I don't think I can do it on my own. Could you help me please?" I give her a nod, and the boys drop their towels and leave the room, shutting the door behind them.

"Do you want to find her some warm clothes?" I suggest to her mum.

She places a hand on my shoulder, as I cradle her wet daughter in my arms and she says with a sad smile, "Tanya. You can call me Tanya

'' I smile back, as she moves to a dresser near the window. She comes back a moment later with cute flannel pajamas covered with little pigs. Tamsyn is still wrapped so tightly in a ball, I don't know where to start. Tanya moves closer and tugs Tamsyn's shoes and socks off while I hold her.

"Tamsyn," I call her, but there's no reaction. Then I remember, my special name for her, got through to her before. Will it work again? "Sweetness," I softly say, but still no reaction.

"Come on Sweetness, come back to me" I plead fiercely. I hear a tiny whimper come from her. I know she can hear me now. I need to draw her out more so I continue talking to her. "It's okay Sweetness. I'm here. I've got you." Her grip on herself slowly loosens and she lets go of her legs and her arms. I rotate her in my arms so it's easier for her mum to take off her clothes. I keep my eyes to the ceiling. She begins with her skirt and underwear, pulling them down her legs and dumps them into a pile on the carpet, not caring it will get wet.

She pulls underwear up Tamsyn's legs then says, "Let's get the top off before I put her pants on otherwise they'll get wet too." She gives me a once over. "Should I see if I can find you some spare clothes too? Your shirt is soaked through." I see the wet material clinging to my chest. Without hesitation, I use one hand to maneuver it off, adding it to the wet pile. I sit down on her bed and position her floppy body so her back is to me. She may be out of it but I want to keep her modesty.

Her mum is holding a dry crop top in her hands so I say, "I'll take off the wet clothes and you quickly put on the dry?" She nods, ready to spring into action. I rest Tamsyn's head against my shoulder and say, "Sweetness, I'm going to remove your wet top okay? Then your mum will put your dry clothes on." She doesn't react. I haven't looked at her face yet but I fear what I will see. Her mum examines Tamsyn's face, takes in her broken daughter and tears fill her eyes, pouring over the edge silently. She's utterly heartbroken.

Trying to distract her, I glide my hands down to the bottom of Tamsyn's shirt and draw the wet material up and away from her body.

Her arms get dragged up as they follow the shirt and I pull her head through then discard the shirt to the wet pile. Her mum's sharp intake of breath shocks me.

Thinking something else is wrong with Tamsyn I say, "What is it?"

Her mum covers her mouth to hide her sniffles and says, "She's lost so much weight. I didn't notice. Too consumed in my own grief, I couldn't see how much my daughter was hurting too."

"Don't worry. We will fix her," I tell Tanya, in a determined voice. I unsnap her bra drawing her mum's attention to our current mission. I lower her straps pulling one arm through at a time, leaving the cups in place. Her mum smiles at me after noticing my efforts of trying to be respectful. I leave Tamsyn's arms up and Tanya threads the crop top down and over her chest, taking the wet bra away at the same time. She grabs the flannel top and does the same, threading her arms through and pulling it down to cover her. I lift Tamsyn's legs one at a time so her mum can get her pants on, then lift her butt so her mum can finish getting them on.

"There we go dear, all dry now," her mum says to the unresponsive girl, I hold in my arms. "I'll take her wet clothes and tell the boys she's decent," her mum says as she gathers the clothes in her arms and heads out the door.

While I have a moment alone with her, I turn her in my arms so she's facing me, straddling my lap. Her legs and arms hang at her sides, slack and motionless. My heart cracks a fraction because she doesn't cling to me. I brace myself in preparation. I bring my eyes to hers and my own fill with tears at what I see. Her once piercing blue eyes are lifeless and emotionless.

I let the tears fall freely down my face as I plead to her, "Please Sweetness, come back to me. I'm sorry if I hurt you today. I wasn't thinking. I need you to come back to me." Wiping the tears from my face, I hold her cheek in my hand while doubt in my abilities to draw her out seep in. Remembering the promise I made to the broken girl at the dock, I take a deep breath and I try again. I rub my thumb back and forth against her cheek. "Sweetness, I know you don't remember but I made a promise to you I'd save you from drowning. Here I am, trying to save you. Please help me save you. Come back to me." With a sharp intake of breath, like she's been starved of air, she draws oxygen into her lungs.

A small amount of life returns to her eyes as they meet mine and the tears fall from both our eyes as she whimpers, "You're here." She wraps her arms tightly around my neck and her legs hug my waist, pulling her as close to me as she can get. I hold her tightly, relief washing over me because she's okay.

I pull away from her a fraction so we can see eye to eye and say, "Tamsyn, I need you to promise me you will never do anything like this again. I wouldn't be able to survive it a second time." She nods and burrows closer to me.

I'm not sure how long we cling to each other, letting our combined tears fall together. A quiet knock sounds on the door and I'm brought back to reality, remembering my friends.

"Come in," I call out to them, and the guys and Tanya come in to see how we are doing. Her mum's relief is evident on her face as she sees more life in her daughter than when she left us. She rushes to her, cups her daughter's face and delivers kisses to it.

"Sorry, I scared you Mum," she says so gently, it's nearly a whisper.

"Don't worry love. I'm sorry too. I was so preoccupied I didn't see how much pain you were in. We will fix this," her mum tells her. The guys creep closer trying to get a glimpse at Tamsyn with their own eyes to see she's back to what she calls normal.

A small "Hi," leaves her lips as she gazes at Rafe and Scott and they're both beaming smiles her way. JP with his head hanging low stays at the back, not wanting to upset her again. Her mum claps her hands together with a great idea forming in her mind.

"I'm going to go order some pizzas for dinner as my way of saying thank you. I don't know what I would have done if you hadn't shown up today," she says, staring at us each individually in the eyes giving us her thanks. As she leaves and goes down stairs to order the food, Rafe picks up the last dry towel left behind. He comes up behind Tamsyn and dries her hair. He locates a scrunchie on her desk, grabs it and secures her damp locks.

"There, now your back won't get wet," he says.

"Thank you," Tamsyn says to him, then she adds, "JP, it wasn't your fault. I was ready to erupt. A lot of things came to a head today and I exploded. Unfortunately, it happened when we were talking. So please don't feel guilty. You were trying to be a good friend and cousin to Tate. I wouldn't want any less from you," she sincerely tells him, her voice still scratchy from all the crying she's done today.

"I shouldn't have gone off at you like that though. I'm sorry," he returns to her. She gives him a small nod, accepting his apology.

After seeing JP, she curiously asks, "What happened to your face?" The bruise around JP's eye is starting to darken as time goes on and it has swollen too.

"It was Scott. He didn't appreciate how I talked to you," he admits, hanging his head in shame. She glances at Scott and a fleeting look of hope passes her face; hope he cares for her. Scott shyly gazes up at her and then away not liking the attention it brought to him. So I change the subject to take the limelight off Scott.

"Do you need anything?" I ask her. With her still in my lap, I'm hoping she doesn't want to move for any reason. I'm more than happy to stay like this forever.

"No. I'm good now," she says, with a slight smile as she squeezes her legs around me tighter.

Scott comes up on the side of me, sitting down to get a good view of her face.

"You scared us T, don't do that again please," he tells her, and my heart warms knowing they care about her as much as I do now. It hasn't been long at all but we've all taken to her so easily and if she wasn't around us anymore I think we would all feel the absence.

"I won't," she promises to him. Rafe takes a seat at her desk and JP ops to sit on the floor by my feet. We sit in a comfortable silence all lost in our own thoughts. My heart once again stitches itself together with the thread that is Tamsyn.

Tate

Twenty minutes later, Tanya comes back into the room and says, "Pizza is here boys. Come downstairs and help yourselves." I don't want to put her down. I know she's safe in my arms and I want to keep her there, away from harm. Even if the harm is coming from herself.

"Let's go eat," she quietly says to me, drawing my thoughts back to the present. She must pick up on my hesitation because as the others file out of the room, the pizza calling to their empty stomachs, she cups my face in both of her vulnerable hands, staring straight into my eyes. "I'm still here, Tate. I'm okay." I stare back at her, searching her eyes for any reason to doubt she's not fully there and find none. She is back but I still don't know how to heal her brokenness. I couldn't do it before so I don't know what makes me think now will be any different. Maybe I'm not the right person for the job? I have already failed once before. As the doubt creeps into my mind, the thoughts overwhelm me and I feel panic take over. No, not now. I can hear my laboured breathing. Tamsyn's eyes shift from trying to reassure me she's alright to worry, as she feels the shift in me.

Still clutching my face she cries, "Tate, what's wrong? What's happening?" I stare up at the ceiling, hoping if I take my eyes off her, it will slow my breathing. Thundering thoughts circle my brain. Will I be able to save her? Was it me that sent her over the edge today? Is she too much like Quinn? Quinn. Damn it. Don't think. Don't think.

I feel the familiar tingle in my hands. I need to get away from her and fast. She's causing me to overload and I can't control myself right now. I quickly shift her off my lap and she stands staring at me at a loss with what to do.

Through blocked ears I hear her scream, "JP, help now." I hear a distant rumble of feet galloping in my direction. I squeeze my eyes shut and focus on my breathing. Come on, let this pass. Contact on my knees has me looking down. JP is crouched in front of me.

"Tate? Can you hear me?" I nod, still not able to catch my breath. I know if I set my eyes on anyone else I will see the pity I dread. "Go for a run bro. You need to run." A run, yes, it might help. "We will take care of Tamsyn, don't worry," he says as he pushes himself up to stand in front of me and drags me to my feet. Once I'm steady, I don't hesitate. I fly out of the room, down the stairs and out the front door. I get lost in the pounding rhythm of my feet hitting the pavement. I feel each step as it takes me further away from my mind and helps the thoughts drift away. My panic subsides and my body takes over, going through the motions I have become so accustomed to, like a second nature.

I'm not entirely sure how much time has passed before my feet lead me back to Tamsyn's house. I stand outside for a minute, catching my breath so I'm ready to face her. Don't think. You can do this. She needs you right now. I enter the house, push my doubts aside and follow the voices I hear coming from the kitchen. All eyes stare at me as I walk in.

"You good now, bro?" JP asks, but I'm not ready to speak so I nod. He hesitantly smiles at me and says, "Cool come eat before Rafe here finishes it all."

"Hey, I'm not the one sitting there hogging all the Supreme to himself," Rafe accuses JP, and they all laugh. I grab a plate and load a few slices on it and sit down next to Tamsyn. She places her frail hand on mine in a gesture of thanks.

"Are you sure you're okay? she quietly asks. I raise my eyes and see the concern shining in her eyes.

"I'm better now. Sorry if I scared you," I tell her, hoping she wasn't too worried because she should be focussing on herself right now.

"Nothing to be sorry for. I'm glad you're alright," she says, giving my hand a squeeze. I notice her plate has one slice of pizza on it so I snag a couple more slices and place them on her plate, hoping she will eat more. She smiles at me and gathers up a slice folding it in half and takes a big bite for my benefit. I can't help but return the smile.

"Dude, do you mind?" Rafe directs my way, and I raise my brows in confusion. "Put a shirt on. Your muscles are distracting me while I eat." Everyone laughs while my cheeks heat up but Tanya saves me by handing me a random black t-shirt and a pair of shorts.

"These belonged to Vince, Tamsyn's dad. You can have a shower after we eat," she sadly says, while handing me the clothes.

"Thank you," I tell her, as I take the clothing from her hands, noticing a slight shake to them. I place my hand on top of hers, giving it a slight squeeze hoping she realises I understand how hard it must be to give away something of her husband's. Her mouth lifts in a tiny smile.

I don't think Tanya has ever catered for a group of teenage boys before as she ordered ten pizzas, three garlic breads and two bottles of Coca-Cola. Although the way Rafe and JP are inhaling the food, she probably estimated right.

As we eat in silence, Tamsyn breaks it by asking, "What time is it?"

"It's after eight," Tanya informs us. "So Tate, I organised with the boys here to have a slumber party," she says cheerily as if it's an everyday occurrence. I cast a look at the boys and they all shrug at me with the smallest hints of smiles on their faces. Even JP. "They've all rung their parents to tell them where they are. So it's all sorted. Boys, once you've finished, you can help me drag some spare mattresses into Tamsyn's room." It doesn't bother her she's invited four teenage guys to bunk in her daughter's room for the night.

"Mum, are you sure about this?" Tamsyn turns, asking her.

With glistening eyes her mum fixes her gaze on Tamsyn and gently says, "I'd feel better if I knew the guys were with you tonight, if that's okay with you?" Tamsyn nods with understanding. She knows she scared her mum so much her mum is worried what she will do in the night if let alone.

We finish off the pizza, surprisingly leaving two untouched which go into the fridge in case we are in need of a midnight snack. Tanya ushers the guys upstairs to help her with the mattresses and puts them to work. I sit with Tamsyn watching her sneakily out of the corner of my eye. She ate two slices of pizza. I guess I should be grateful she's eaten anything at all considering the day she's had. She must be tired after the day's events. Thinking back over the past twenty-four hours, I can't believe all that's happened. It's like one big roller coaster, jutting and jarring us from every angle possible. I hear the guys' laughter from the lounge and it drags me and Tamsyn from our seats. We walk in there to investigate and find Rafe and Scott both holding a side of the T.V intending to carry it upstairs, I presume.

"What's going on?" Tamsyn asks them.

"We are following Tanya's instructions. She wants us to set it up in the room so we can Netflix and chill," Scott informs her. Scott's revelation has Rafe laughing in hysterics at Tanya's use of lingo.

"She's down with the four-one-one apparently," Rafe says, which brings a smile to Tamsyn's face. Her smile is all that matters. They continue to lug the huge T.V. up the stairs, maneuvering it as they go.

"There's a bathroom down here Tate where you can shower," Tamsyn says, leading me down the hall to the side of the kitchen. I follow her with her dad's clothes in my hand. "Here you go," she says as she pushes the door open. It's identical to the one upstairs but this one at least still has the door attached. "Do you need anything else?" she asks, peering into my eyes. Can she hear my own silent screams I wonder?

"No, I'll be fine," I tell her. She gives my hand a squeeze.

"I don't want to make you uncomfortable or anything but JP said you've been having panic attacks for a while now." She must see the worry cross my face. Did he spill my secrets? She reassures me, "He didn't tell us why they happen or anything, but if you ever want to talk, I want you to know I'm here." I calmly draw a breath in. My secrets are still safe. I grasp her neck and pull her into me, laying a soft kiss on her forehead.

"Thanks, Sweetness," I say. "I'll meet you in your room when I'm done," I say, smiling at her as she walks away when I close the door.

I stand under the water, letting it pelt down on me and regain control over myself. Maybe I've been silly to think it was a good idea trying to help her. She's making me lose control. Don't think. Don't think. Don't think. I shut down my mind so I can focus on getting through the night. She's had a hard day. Focus on her, I tell myself. I shut the water off and change into the unfamiliar clothes, my feet leading me up the stairs towards her.

When I enter, I take in the room. They've lined three single mattresses in a row to form one big bed on the floor. All covered with sheets, pillows and blankets like a real slumber party set up.

Her mum joins us in the packed room a few minutes later with hands full of junk food. She's carrying bags of chips, chocolate, lollies and biscuits. I notice JP and Rafe's eyes light up with glee at the prospect of stuffing their faces with all those delicious treats. Her mum dumps the load of goods onto the mattresses and then goes to exit the room.

"Enjoy yourself kids. I'm right down the hall, if you need anything," she says to me and the guys, with a hidden meaning. If we need her help with Tamsyn, we know where to find her. "And leave the door open, please," she says, with a small smile directed my way. I'm guessing she can see my feelings for her daughter written all over my face. She hooks the door back on her exit as JP grabs the remote, scrolling through the movies finding one for us to watch.

"Tamsyn, any ideas on what we should watch?" he asks, flicking his eyes her way.

"Whatever you want is fine. I'm tired so I'll probably be asleep soon," she tells him. The boys all kick off their shoes and socks. Rafe takes his school shirt off while the other two keep their shirts on. Since they've been trying to track down Tamsyn since school finished, they haven't been home to change. They all pick a mattress and get comfortable, leaving me there with nowhere to go.

Tamsyn whispers to me, "Aren't they adorable?" I try seeing them from her point of view. It must be weird to her having three huge guys all set up on her floor, ready to watch a movie and sleep over. She takes a few steps to her bed and gets under the covers then looks up at me through her lashes. She doesn't say anything as she pats the side of her bed. I smile at her invitation and get under the covers. We both move our pillows behind our backs to sit up and watch the movie. JP chooses some action flick, but my thoughts are too absorbed in the fact I'm in a bed with Tamsyn.

She's different now to how she was this morning. She started today off with a huge genuine smile and now she's ending it a lot more broken than she probably expected to be. She must sense my eyes on her as her gaze leaves the T.V and comes to me.

A single tear drops down her cheek. I wipe it away with my thumb, keeping my hand there to cup her cheek. She closes her eyes and turns her hand into my touch, craving the connection. The boys' laughter comes from the floor. I'd forgotten they were there for a minute, too engrossed in Tamsyn. They're so focussed on the movie; they don't pay any attention to us. It's been long enough without her in my arms; I need to have her there so my body will be at peace. I drop my hand from her face, grab her waist and pull her back into my chest. Turning us on to our sides so she's moulded into me, I cuddle my arms around her, one under her head and the other draped across her waist pulling her as close to me as I can. Her hand rests on my arm, clinging to me, needing me as much as I need her at this moment. She fits perfectly like she's made for me. I can't help it. I take a deep inhale of her neck, needing the fix. She's still here and she's okay, I tell myself, trying to ease the ache in my chest.

Her breathing evens out, so before she falls to sleep I whisper, "Goodnight, Sweetness," delivering a small kiss to the side of her bare neck making her shiver. With a smile upon my face, I let sleep take over me. I'm not frightened of the dreams plaguing me and causing me nothing but pain. I am at peace for a fleeting moment in time, because I have her in my arms. Even if she is a possible trigger for me, at this moment in time, there's no place in the world I would rather be.

Don't Think. Just Breathe.

Chapter 13

Tamsyn

wake up surrounded by warmth. A weight is pressed against my back and hot breath kisses my neck. Slowly awareness dawns on me and I remember flashes of yesterday. Tate. The guys. Pizza. Tate's warm arm still holds me close to his chest like he has all night. His other arm is still under my neck with my head resting on it, using it as a pillow. I hear snores coming from the floor. I let their kindness and worry for me seep into me. They came for me. They saved me last night from myself. I don't know where I'd be if they hadn't; especially Tate. I haven't done anything to deserve his kindness, but still he gives it to me without asking for anything in return.

He scared me with his panic attack. What tortures him so much it causes extreme panic like that? My poor sweet boy. The thought has me snuggling in closer to him. His leg is positioned across my hip, pushing me into the bed as if he was worried I might disappear in the night and wanted to stop me from leaving. As I wriggle to get closer to him, I notice his breath changes. It speeds up as he realises I'm awake.

"Sweetness?" he whispers into the dark. My whole body tingles with the use of my name. I don't dare answer though trying to feign sleep. "Sweetness?" he whispers again, this time granting me a soft kiss to the side of my neck. This time I can't ignore it, not when he's playing dirty. I giggle quietly. He uses his arms to twist me around so

I'm facing him. I still rest on his arm which now cradles me close to him, wrapping around my back. Pulling my head to his chest, he drapes his other arm around me. I place my leg between his, wanting to close the distance as much as possible. "Hi," he whispers into my ear.

I lift my head gazing up at him, while he peers down at me and say, "Hi," back.

"How are you feeling?" he asks, always worried about me.

"Better than yesterday, that's for sure. What about you?" I tell him, because it's the truth.

"I'm good. Do you think you're up to school or are you going to miss today?" he asks me. I hadn't thought about it. A day to stay at home, resting and collecting my thoughts sounds good.

"I might miss today. I don't think I'm up to being around many people. Plus I don't think I would be able to concentrate much at school."

"It sounds like a good idea. I'll miss you though," he says, as he brushes the hair from my forehead, tucking it behind my ear. Bringing his forehead to mine, he rests it there. We both breathe and as we do, our breaths sync with each other, breathing as one. I want to drift off back to sleep in Tate's warm embrace but my mum has other ideas. Knocking on the door has me and Tate pulling away from each other quickly. I hear a few grunts and groans from the floor, signalling the boys are waking up from my mum's intrusion into their sleep.

"Time to get up boys, if you want to get to school on time," she yells loudly, making sure she wakes the sleepy stragglers on the floor.

"We're up," I hear JP say, yawning loudly from his place down below.

"Would you boys like some breakfast before you go?" my mum asks them.

"No, we're fine Tanya. We will get going so we aren't late. Thanks for letting us stay the night," JP says, thanking her.

"I should thank you for staying. It took a weight off my mind knowing you were here too," she says, with a misty smile. The boys get up and try to start cleaning the makeshift beds but my mum won't have it, shooing them out the door before they can do anything. Tate lingers in bed with me, reluctant to leave.

"You better go, you don't want to be late," I tell him unenthusiastically, not wanting him to go.

"You have a good day resting," he says, with a small smile. Leaning up on his elbow he bends down and plants a kiss to my forehead then flings the covers back. Grabbing his shoes and socks, Tate gives me a sad smile as he leaves the room to join the others. I can hear them thanking my mum again as they leave. The loud closing of the front door signifies they've gone.

My mum comes back into my room and asks, "Do you feel up to going to school today?" I shake my head, already having made up my mind to stay home. She sits down on the side of my bed and I can tell she's got something on her mind. "Do you want to talk about anything?" she asks me but again I shake my head. "It's fine dear, you don't have to talk to me but I think you need to talk to someone. You can't bottle this stuff in because yesterday was not good for either of us. I want you to see a grief counsellor or a therapist. I think I could probably benefit from a grief counsellor myself. So, I'll do some research today, shall I?" she asks, with hope in her voice.

"Okay Mum, sounds good," I tell her. I don't want her to worry about me any more than she needs to. I think talking to someone would help me.

"I should probably ring someone to fix the bathroom door too. You should have seen Tate in action. He kicked it right off its hinges like a dashing fireman," she says. So Tate broke the door. I was curious but I didn't want to ask.

She adjusts herself, getting a bit more comfortable on my bed and looking at her face, I see a mischievous grin spread across it.

"Soooo, those boys are delightful, aren't they?" she says, and I know exactly where this is headed.

"Yes Mum, they are," I try to tell her, giving away as little information as possible.

"When did you become friends with them?" Her nosiness is in full steam now and I don't think I can stop the train.

"Recently, so not long," I tell her honestly, because it hasn't been long at all. I don't know if I would have classed JP as a friend before yesterday.

She continues with her inquisition and gets to the question she wanted the answer to all along, "Are you and Tate an item? I thought you were still with Blake?" And there it is; the reason for all her questioning. I let out a frustrated breath, because when I think of Blake it makes me mad and annoyed. She senses my frustration and places a hand on my legs which are snuggled under the blankets. "What is it dear?"

Of their own volition, the words come out of my mouth in an unexpected frenzy, "I found out yesterday Blake has been seeing Leyla behind my back for a few months now, three to be exact. I don't know why he didn't break up with me first. My so called friends are bitches behind my back. They made the message clear yesterday. To be honest, it doesn't matter as it hasn't been the same with me and Blake for a while now. We've been over except neither one of us officially ended it."

She sits still, taking it all in then says, "So how does Tate come into the picture?"

"He was an unexpected surprise. He moved in with his aunt and uncle shortly before school started this year. He was new to the school and didn't have many friends. For some reason, he could see how much

I was struggling when no one else could and tried to help me," I say, dropping my head not wanting to make mum feel guilty.

"I'm glad he was there for you honey. I don't know what to say about Blake and Leyla. Trust your gut though, it will always lead you in the right direction," she says warmly. I think she's taken a liking to Tate. She liked all the boys, which is nice in a weird way.

"Do you know what caused his panic attack?" she asks with concern. I shake my head not having a clue. Done with her enquiries, she says "Did you want to do anything today or get some rest?"

"Rest. I might go back to sleep for a bit if it's okay with you? It was a long day yesterday."

She smiles at me as she gets up, running her hand over my hair. "It's fine dear, you get some rest." She leans forward kissing my head and walks to the door closing it on her way out. I do want to get some sleep, so I get up and hunt through my school bag locating my phone. It's battery is low, so I plug it into the charger. No calls or texts from my so called friends so they must not have heard about my freak out yesterday. I send Blake a message, telling him not to bother picking me up today as I'm sick and not going to school. I wish I could text Tate, missing him already but I still don't have his number. Sighing, I put my phone on vibrate, hop back into bed and go back through the conversation I had with JP when Tate left during his panic attack.

Tate sits there and I sense the moment he changes. His chest is rising and falling so fast, trying to catch a breath. I've never witnessed a panic attack before so it scares me not knowing what is wrong with him. A wall goes up between us and I can't break through the barrier. I'm so helpless. He hastily removes me from his lap like he can't get away fast enough from me. Was it something I did? I scream for JP and he comes barrelling in with worry dripping from his face. He knows exactly what to do to help Tate.

After Tate shoots off outside, JP explains to us about Tate, "Tate suffers from panic attacks. It's not my business to tell you what the main cause is. I'm sure Tate will tell you in his own time. He does get triggered though." He glances at me quickly before he averts his stare and I wonder if it's me, was I the trigger this time? "He can usually get himself under control by focussing on his breathing exercises but other times, running helps. You can never tell which will work but if you notice them happening, try to get him to calm his breathing. It usually does the trick," he finishes. The guys are as worried as I am about Tate. My mum is a bit shaken too. Tate's a big guy and to see him vulnerable is heartbreaking.

"Come on everyone. I'm sure Tate wouldn't want us dwelling on it so let's head downstairs to eat." Mum studies my face before she walks out the door with Rafe and Scott behind her. I hear her say, "Boys, I need your help organising something." This leaves me alone with JP.

"Will Tate be alright?" I ask JP, before he follows behind them. He turns to me with a sad expression.

"I hope so," he says.

"Was it me triggering him, this time?" I can't help but ask.

"To be honest, I'm not sure. He isn't usually forthcoming about them. But I will say this. This is exactly the reason why I wanted you to be careful with him. You both aren't in the right headspace at the moment. I worry it won't be good for either of you to lean on the other too much." I sway on my feet and JP comes to my side, holding me around the waist. "Are you okay? Let me help you down the stairs. I hope I didn't upset you, it wasn't my intention."

"No you didn't. It's been a big day and it's taken it out of me," I lie, as we slowly shuffle to the kitchen.

"I am sorry about earlier too," JP says, apologising again.

"It's all forgotten now," I say, trying to ease his guilt.

I replay the conversation over and over in my head. I must have done something I'm unaware of which set Tate off last night. I wish I could help him like he helps me. I snuggle under the covers, trying to put my mind at ease so sleep will come.

______________________________Tate______________________________

JP drops Rafe and Scott off at their houses to get ready, saying we will be back to pick them up shortly. We decided to ride to school together today. After last night something has shifted. Our already close bond is tighter. Being there for Tamsyn has cemented our friendship in a way I wasn't expecting and this includes Tamsyn. I don't know what would have happened if we hadn't gone to her house. The image of her frail body being pelted by freezing water still burns in the back of my mind. I've pushed it aside but it still creeps to the front giving me a glimpse before I manage to push it away again.

We arrive back at JP's house, and his mum and dad are there at the kitchen table eating breakfast. They have usually left for work by now so I suspect they want to talk to us.

"Boys," my uncle Todd greets us.

"Hey," me and JP say in unison. They put down their coffee mugs, giving us their full attention. Sharon turns to us and I can sense a talk is coming.

"First off, is Tanya's daughter alright?" she asks, and we nod. "Good," she says with a smile. "From what JP told me on the phone yesterday, it sounded like she needed your help. I'm glad you could be there for her and everything worked out." We nod again not wanting to engage in talk about the situation. "Secondly, what happened to your face John?" she asks her son, taking in the bruising. It's much more prominent after having the night to develop.

"I deserved it," is all he says to her, and funnily enough she accepts the brief explanation, knowing how her son can be.

"Last question," this statement comes from Todd, and he's staring straight at me so I know I'm not going to like whatever is about to come out of his mouth. "Are you sure this girl is good for you right now Tate? From what I've heard about her, she sounds like Quinn."

With the mention of the name I try to avoid at all costs, the air is squeezed out of my lungs and my ears block out all sound. My body takes me to my safe space of complete numbness. In this space I don't think, I don't feel. I don't exist. It's my body's coping mechanism, protecting me from what hurts me most in the world so I block everything around me out. If I can block it out, it can't hurt me. This is how I stay, until my mind senses it's safe to come out. When I come out of the fog of numbness, I'm thrusted back into reality with three voices yelling at each other.

"What the hell, Dad?"

"Todd, we talked about it. You weren't supposed to mention her."

"I've got his best interests at heart. If this girl reminds him of her, it can't be healthy for him to be so invested in her."

"STOP!!" I scream at them. All three sets of eyes stare at me, anxiously waiting, not sure what I will do next.

"Tate," my uncle says.

I push past him saying, "Don't."

On my way out of the room I hear JP say, "Leave it, Dad." I go to the bathroom, strip Vince's clothes off and get under the hot shower spray, turning it up hotter so it's scalding my skin. I need the heat to burn my soul clean of all my pain, threatening to surface. I managed to keep it contained last night because JP told me to run. Tamsyn makes me feel what I don't want to. For the life of me, I can't bear to stay away from her though. I can handle it, can't I? I stare at the wall, letting the water rain down on me. Don't think. Don't think. Don't think! I let the emptiness consume me again. Numb is what I need now. Numb keeps me safe.

Riding to school with the guys, I've managed to get myself into a state of detachment. I'm here but my mind isn't; keeping the hurt at bay for as long as I need it. I know Tamsyn won't be at school today so I don't need to pull myself out of this state. I can cope better this way.

I'm distant all day. Going through the motions, letting my mind recover and take the rest it needs. I've made it all the way to lunch time without knowing what is going on, my body taking over for me. I'm in cruise control. I'm glad the guys haven't pushed to know about my episode last night. It's something at least. As we sit out in the sun in our usual seats, the guys' voices drag me out of the haze back to the present.

"Did you get her number so you could check on her?" Rafe asks me, and I shake my head, forgetting I don't have her number.

"Do you think she'll be alright?" Scott asks me, and I know the others are staring at me too, gauging my reaction. They're talking about Tamsyn.

"Yeah, I think she will be. We'll be there to help her too, right?" I question them, hoping we are all on the same page when it comes to her.

"Definitely."

"Sure."

"Of course," are the three answers I get from them.

"Has anyone mentioned her outburst yesterday?" I ask them, since I've been zoned out most of the day and haven't paid attention.

"I've heard a few people talk about her and JP arguing but not about what was said so they can't have been listening as intently as we thought," Scott says.

"More people are talking about the fact Scott punched JP. Now they think there's some weird love triangle going on," Rafe says with a cheeky grin on his face, trying to contain his laughter. I chuckle at him and it has Scott and JP joining in too. They carry on cracking jokes with light banter through lunch distracting me. I miss Tamsyn though and having human bio next isn't helping.

As the bell rings signalling the end of lunch, we clear our trays, say goodbye to JP and rush to the science labs so we're not late. Entering the room and seeing her empty seat leaves me disappointed. I know she's at home but it's as if my heart still hoped she might magically appear. I take my seat as Ms. Chadwick informs us we are going to continue learning about the structure of the eye and all the functions. I grab my things out of my bag and psych myself up to pay attention. The least I could do is get notes for Tamsyn so she doesn't miss out on too much. I flip my book open to the next blank page and what I see sends warmth straight to my heart. Tamsyn's written her number, wanting me to have it. She must have done this Monday night when she had my book. The fact warms my heart more. I've worried about how she was all day so I wait no longer to text her. I grab my phone out of my pocket and programme her number into it, then text her.

Tate: Sweetness, u ok?

I hold my phone under my desk hoping she will reply straight away. After a few minutes with no reply, I switch it to vibrate and put it in my pocket so I won't miss it if she does text. I'm distracted the whole class waiting for a text but still nothing comes through. It's not until near the end of class when my pocket vibrates. Eagerness has me whipping my phone out post haste.

Sweetness: Hi Tate, u found my number? I'm ok. Just woke up from a nap.

I quickly type out a reply but another text comes through before I send it.

Sweetness: How's school?

Tate: Yes, it was a sneaky but welcome surprise.

Tate: Would b better if u were here. Human bio not the same without u.

Sweetness: I will def b there 2moro :)

The bell rings for the end of class so I throw my stuff in my bag. As we maneuver down the halls, I let Rafe and Scott know Tamsyn left her number in my book, I texted her and she was okay. They're happy to hear that. I won't be able to text her back now though as Mr. Barnes has a no phone policy. I don't want to risk my phone getting confiscated if he catches me with it. Not when it's my connection to Tamsyn now.

I catch a ride home with JP and manage to last all through dinner and completing my homework before the urge to text Tamsyn wins. I don't want to bother her too much, in case she's sleeping, so decide to keep it sweet and simple.

Tate: Missed you today. Cant wait 2 c u 2moro. Dream sweet xo

Chapter 14

Tamsyn

After a good day and night's rest, I wake up refreshed and I'm ready to get back to school. I need to fix this Blake situation. The sooner, the better. I don't want to see him this morning so I text him not to worry about picking me up again. After telling him I was sick yesterday, all I got was one text saying okay. That was it. He's not a good boyfriend. Not to worry, because today I am breaking up with him. No point in dragging it out any longer.

I spend a good twenty minutes in bed, giving myself a huge pep talk. At the end of it, I feel as though I could take on the world. It all comes crashing down when I put my uniform on, my mum washed for me. It's the same uniform I had absently gotten into the shower with on. Realisation hits me, going straight through my chest. I unzip my skirt pocket, holding onto the smallest glimmer of hope but the last shred quickly evaporates when I pull out clumps of mushed up paper. Tate's star. My lifeline. It's gone. I'd forgotten I had it in my pocket. I can't believe it. I got in the shower with it in there and ruined it. I drop to the floor, clinging to the clumps. It's ruined. Exactly how I feel; destroyed and beyond repair. Every time I take a step forward, instead of taking two steps back, I'm thrown backwards over a cliff, trying to cling on with my bare fingers to save me and pull myself to safety. When I think I might be safe, something comes along to take the safety away. Wet tears drip onto my carpet. I've lost another piece of myself.

This was the first note Tate gave to me and now it's gone. Sadness wells up inside me.

'DING DING' I hear a text notification sound come from my phone. It's probably Blake replying to the one I sent. I crawl to my bedside table and grab my phone. My heart skips a beat at the name on my screen. Tate. I open the message:

T: Good morning Sweetness. Me and JP are waiting outside to give you a ride to school so whenever you're ready :)

I stand up, wiping my tears away and stumble to the window and peek through my curtains. There's JP's car like he said. I quickly finish getting ready, walk into the bathroom and splash cold water on my face. It's blotchy but I'm hoping they won't notice. Grabbing my things, I race down stairs and call out to my mum in the kitchen.

"I don't need you to give me a ride now, Mum. Tate and JP are outside waiting for me," I tell her.

"That's wonderful dear. Glad you've got great friends like them," she says, with a huge smile on her face.

"Bye Mum," I say, waving as I rush out the door, closing it behind me. As I get to the car, I notice Tate isn't in the passenger seat next to JP, he's sitting in the back by himself.

"Come sit by me," he calls to me through his open window. Opening the car door I hop in next to him.

"Hi," he says, when I look up at him.

"Hi," I shyly reply back.

"Hey Tamsyn. You feeling a bit better today?" JP asks, from the front seat as he pulls away from the curb.

"Yeah a little" I tell him. But the all too perceptive Tate knows something is wrong. I've buckled myself in by the window so he buckles himself into the middle seat, wanting to be close to me and to offer us some privacy. He doesn't want JP to hear us over the music. He grasps my chin pulling me to him and he doesn't have to ask. I can see the question in his eyes along with his concern.

"I'm okay," I tell him. And because there's something about him which makes me blurt the truth without meaning to.

"You remember the star you drew for me? I ask, and he nods in reply, waiting for me to continue.

"Well I had it in my pocket the other night when I...when ...umm got in the shower." I stammer, as I don't want to burden him with those memories again. Understanding crosses his face.

"Is it ruined?" he asks, and my lips quiver as I nod. "Hey. It's alright. I've got an idea," he says, as he's digging in his bag for something. Pulling out a black pen he grabs my hand, twisting it and drawing on it below my thumb. It tickles as he makes the little marks.

It doesn't take long at all and as we are pulling into the car park he says, "Done." He turns my hand over for me to see and there staring back at me is my star, shrouded by darkness but this one is different. One edge of the star is not connected and there's no darkness surrounding it. It's not a big gap at all but big enough to notice. I raise my brows and he smiles wide, leaning so close to my ear I can feel his warm breath and says, "It's where you start letting the light in, little one." My heart melts into a puddle on the car floor. Could he be any more perfect? A single tear escapes my eye and he brushes it gently away from my face saying, "That's plenty of tears for today. You've got this," giving my hand a gentle squeeze before we exit the car.

Breathe. You've got this. Breathe. I tell myself as I walk the halls avoiding people's eyes, staring at the ground. I check my phone to see what the time is and notice the icon says I have an unread message. I scroll through until I find it. It's from Tate. It says it was sent last night when I was sleeping. There must have been a delay in me receiving it.

His sweet message gives me a burst of energy and I am ready to take on the day. I can do this.

The day is uneventful until lunch time. No one has said anything to me about the other day. It's obviously not big news or else they've got something more exciting to talk about. Tate said he would see me at lunch time, if I'd like to sit with them. I didn't hesitate; I told him I would be there.

I'm lined up, grabbing a tray when I hear a familiar voice say, "Hey T, haven't seen you much today. How's it going?"

"Hey Scott, I'm doing the best I can. How are you?' I say with a smile, at his little nickname he has for me now.

"I'm good. Do you wanna walk with me outside? I think the guys are already out there, stuffing their faces like usual."

I laugh as I say, "Yes, please." I grab my usual sandwich and apple but the chocolate muffin was so good the other day, so I grab one of those too. Tate will be proud of me.

Scott, carrying his overflowing tray, is beside me as we start walking to the door leading outside when I hear, "Tammy," being called. I turn in the direction it came from. It's Blake. Ugh. Seeing his face makes my blood boil.

I turn back to Scott quickly saying, "Wait for me," as I march towards Blake's table.

Leyla's screeching voice pierces me to my core when she wails loudly, trying to cause a scene, "Ewww please don't tell me the rumours are true and you're getting it on with Snotty Scotty over there," and it's all I need to erupt at her.

"Firstly, his name is Scott, you bitch. You don't need to make fun of him, to make yourself feel better," I scream loud enough, the whole cafeteria has gone silent. Everyone looks our way, intrigued to see what will happen next. She tries to talk but I hold up my hand in her put off face, halting whatever she was going to say.

"Secondly, he's been a better friend to me in the last few days than all of you have been to me in years," I address the whole table, spinning my finger around to indicate all of them. Leyla, Chloe, Parker and Blake. They all sit there in stunned silence.

"Thirdly, Blake, this one's for you. You and I are done. We haven't been a proper couple in ages so let's put a pin in it and pop this shit show we call a relationship."

"Tammy?" He stares at me confused, not knowing what the hell is happening. I started going off at Leyla then turned on him.

"Lastly," I add, "If I am with Scott, it's none of your business. I can tell you, he would be a total upgrade from you." And with that, I move to stand next to Scott who's grinning ear to ear, enjoying me putting them in their places. To hammer the final nail in the coffin so Blake can't try and pull off the good guy act anymore, I turn back to them.

"Oh, and I heard congratulations are in order on your three month anniversary Leyla and Blake. So congrats." I spin around, addressing the whole shocked cafeteria and a pale Leyla and Blake, "My dad dies and you start screwing my best friend." There's more than a few oohs and sharp intakes of breath at the juicy piece of information. "So screw you all. We are done." I add, turning on my heels and march out the door to my new friends with the gleeful Scott, hot on my trail.

My hands are shaking as I sit down, with the three unaware boys who didn't witness my outburst. Scott sits there with the stupidest grin on his face, so it isn't long before they are asking him what he's so chuffed about.

"You guys missed the greatest show ever. Tamsyn kicked some serious butt," he tells them enthusiastically.

"What happened?" All three of them direct their questions at me.

"Before the incident in the car park the other day, I overheard Leyla tell Chloe how she's been seeing Blake behind my back for the last three months," I inform them. Tate and JP jump up ready for a fight.

"That piece of shit, I'll kill him," Tate says enraged, and he's half way back to the door before I get to him. Blocking his way and putting both my hands on his arms, I put all my strength into pushing him so he will stop. He looks down at me breathing hard, trying to calm himself down.

"Hey, it's fine. I took care of it. I broke up with him and dumped my useless friends in the process," I tell him.

"They're your friends though. They should have treated you better," he says, still angry.

"Honestly, they were pretty useless friends. Like I said, you guys have been way better friends to me in the last few days than they have in years, so don't sweat it. I have you now. I mean I have you guys; all of you. So I don't need them," I stumble over my words, while my face turns bright red. This has Tate grinning happily as he tries not to laugh at what I said. He leans in and lowers his voice so the guys can't hear him.

"Yes, you do indeed have us. I mean, you have me," he says, staring at me dead in the eye, with the perfect smile of his.

"Let's go sit down now," I quietly tell him, and he leads us back to our table.

As we sit down Scott says, "So T here, pretty much told everyone me and her are a couple."

"What?" Tate screeches loudly. His outburst draws our attention to him and we can't help but laugh at his shocked expression.

Scott lets him in on what was said, "She was defending me, man. Told them I'd be a way better upgrade than Blake." Which has the whole table laughing again. Then behind his hand, like he thinks he's being discreet but he's being blatantly obvious, he says to Tate, "Don't worry, we all know whose girl she is." He gives Tate a couple of winks, for good measure. I swear my face burns up more. I want to crawl under the table and hide. Tate gives me a shy smile which I can't help but return.

"I'm proud of you girl, it must have taken a lot of courage to do that today, in front of everyone too. Especially after the last few days you've had," Rafe sincerely says.

"Someone told me to start letting the light in. So I was following his advice," I say, smiling at Tate quickly then I pick up my muffin and break some off, eating it. I feel lighter than I was this morning.

______________________________Tate______________________________

I'm blown away by Tamsyn. I can't believe she stood up for herself like that. It's amazing. She's amazing; especially after all she has been through lately. Blake, the prick. He better not come near me. I don't know if I'll be able to handle my rage if he gets within swinging distance. Me, Scott and Tamsyn are headed to English now. As we enter, Tamsyn scans the room focussing on her seat down the back.

Scott notices her hesitation and says, "You know T, I can move over and make room for you between me and Tate if you like?" She beams up at him.

"Thanks Scott. That would be great." So that's how we sit, same as in human bio but in reverse. Leyla and Chloe walk in and we are already seated.

Leyla trying to win back some pride says, "Guess you've joined the loser squad now," directing it at Tamsyn.

Tamsyn ignores her but surprisingly it is Penny who chimes in with, "Shut up Leyla, we all know who the loser here is and it ain't Tamsyn. Who sleeps with their best friend's boyfriend?" and it has half the class glaring at Leyla with revulsion, the other half could care less. She and her sidekick Chloe slink away to their chairs at the back of the class and we don't hear another peep out of them. Tamsyn turns to Penny and offers a smile. I see Penny nod her head at Tamsyn in acknowledgement for sticking up for her. She could use someone else in her corner right now.

After English, the three of us walk together to human bio. Even though I got to sit by her in English, human bio is different. More special for some reason, unbeknown to me. I can see on Tamsyn's face it's been a long day emotionally for her. I know the feeling. Sometimes you get so overloaded with feelings when you've been numb for so long, it drains you of your energy. I don't say anything when she lays her head on her arms; I think she could do with the reprieve for a while. I saw her face light up when I drew my star on her this morning so I decide to draw it again on some paper so she can keep it in her pocket for when she needs it. She was devastated this morning when she said it got wrecked. I flip to a page in my book and rip two equal bits out. On one piece, I draw the original star which got ruined, and on the other, I draw the new one I drew on her hand this morning; the one letting the light in. I think she needs it more than the other right now. But I'll let her decide what she needs.

I don't want to wait to give them to her like I do with my notes on Fridays so I fold them up and copy her pose. I fold my arms and lay them on the desk next to hers then put my head down and concentrate on the board. Our arms are touching and it appears as if we are both resting. Luckily no one can see our hands. I sneakily wiggle my fingers with the notes in them and slide them into her hand. She grabs at the notes. Her next move has my heart beating a million miles a minute. She twists her hand so the notes fall to her desk then she's threading her fingers through mine, grasping my hand tightly. Our private moment goes unseen and it's how we stay for the remainder of the class; clinging to each other's fingers with no one the wiser. As the bell goes for the end of class, we release, giving each other a gentle squeeze before we let go. Lifting our heads off our arms, we smile at each other. Tamsyn remembering the notes, picks them up, opening them and her smile grows as she sees what they are. Unzipping her pocket, she places them in there delicately, like they mean the world to her. This small gesture makes my heart fix a bit of itself; her small smile is responsible.

I told Tamsyn we would drop her home after school, so she should meet us in the car park after her last class. It's what me and JP are doing now, waiting at his car for her to show up. In the distance, I catch a glimpse of chocolate brown hair but then it gets lost in the crowd of students trying to make their way home for the day. I search the students meandering through the cars but I can't see her.

"JP can you see her? I saw a glimpse of her then she disappeared," I yell across the hood of the car. He helps me search the crowd of students for her.

A few moments pass and then he yells back, "There," pointing her way. What I see has my rage returning and before I know it, my feet are dragging me towards her. Towards where Blake has her cornered. I sense JP's presence at my back, ready to spring into action if need be

As I get closer I hear Blake's vile mouth yelling at her, "How could you do that? In front of the whole school too? What did you expect me to do? Wait around for you to snap out of your weird daydreaming fog of grief you are always in lately? You've been so selfish. I have needs, you know? You're such a frigid b**..."

'CRACK' My fist connects perfectly with his nose, breaking it before he could finish his statement. He falls backwards onto the pavement clutching his bloodied face, whimpering into his hands.

I lean over him, my voice thick with venom, "You come at her again and it won't be your nose I break. Got it?" I can tell he's about to say some snide remark from the disdain dripping off his face. This lasts a moment before his face turns a pale white as he looks over my shoulder.

"He asked you a question," I hear JP say.

"You'll have all of us to deal with," Scott chimes in.

"I've always wanted an excuse to break your pretty face," Rafe tells him, cracking his knuckles. Blake visibly gulps. I'm surprised he hasn't shit himself with the way we all stare him down. You can practically see the anger seeping from our pores.

"Got it," he says, before he pushes off the ground, running away to his car with blood pouring down his face.

My first thought as he disappears is Tamsyn, so I turn to her and she's visibly shaking. I pull her into my arms, holding her close. The guys make a semicircle around me so I can make sure she's alright.

"He won't bother you anymore but if he does, we will deal with him," Rafe says to her. Her shaking lessens, the more I hold her.

"Where did you guys come from?" I direct my question towards Scott and Rafe.

"We were walking out together and saw Blake yelling at someone but couldn't see who," Scott says.

"Then we saw your enraged ass firing across the car park like a bullet. We guessed it was Tamsyn so we ran over. Got here in time to see you clock him," Rafe adds, trying not to laugh. I roll my eyes at him.

"I wasn't that bad, was I?" I ask, because I don't know. I saw Tamsyn unsafe, saw red and my body took over.

"Well, you did nearly knock about five people down as you charged through them," Rafe throws back at me. He's clearly finding this situation way too amusing so I choose to ignore him.

"Let's get you to the car, Sweetness," I say, focussing on her. I sling my arm over her shoulder, drawing her tiny form into my side. Scott takes her bag off her shoulder and carries it for her then he links hands with her. If my eyes could shoot lasers, I would sear Scott's hand off. I know he's doing it as a friend but my heart doesn't know the difference.

My heart doesn't like the fact someone else is touching her. Touching her, how I was a few short hours ago.

As we get to the car, JP asks the guys if they need a ride home. They had both been dropped off by their parents this morning so they're more than happy for a ride. We all pile into the car. I take the middle seat and have Tamsyn sit by the window because my caveman tendencies are in full swing. I don't want the guys touching her if I can help it. I need to get this jealousy under control. Rafe jumps in the front and Scott is on my other side. He stares out the window with a smirk on his face. He knows exactly why I'm sitting in the middle. My irrational behaviour has become their entertainment. Tamsyn, unaware of my jealousy, takes my hand in hers, keeping it from view of the others and hiding it by my legs. The gesture has my heart loosening its hold on all the jealousy and rage I felt earlier. Instead I focus on the softness of her precious hands.

"Are you guys excited about the Team Building day tomorrow?" Scott says.

"Oh, I forgot. It's free dress aye?" I ask. It had slipped my mind with all the commotion after school.

"Yeah it is. Any day where we don't have to wear these horrible ties is a day to embrace," Rafe says, as he loosens the tie around his neck.

"I've heard it's a fun day from previous seniors. They try to get us all in a good mood at the beginning of the school year. It's a free pass to fool around and play games," Scott tells us.

"Anything beats going to class," Tamsyn chimes in, and I give her hand a discrete squeeze. We drop Scott off first, then Tamsyn. As she exits the car, I run my thumb back and forth over the back of her hand in a quiet goodbye. She smiles sweetly at me exiting the car, and making her way up the path to her front door, disappearing behind it.

I told Tamsyn yesterday we would pick her up for school in the mornings from now on. The announcement made her very happy. I've decided to wear faded light blue jean shorts and a plain black muscle tee today. JP is wearing full length dark blue denim jeans and a white t-shirt with a lion print on the front. I'm sweating from seeing him in those jeans. It's too hot for full length pants but to each their own I guess. As we wait outside Tamsyn's place for her, me in the back seat again, I can't help but let my mind wander, wondering what she might wear. My imagination was nowhere close to the magnificent sight of the real thing. She bounds down the path from her house with her straightened chocolate hair swaying behind her. That alone has my heart rate increasing as it's a rare sight to see her with her hair down. It's my personal favourite as it makes her more gorgeous than she already is. She's wearing a thin strapped baby pink singlet which hangs off her frame. Short dark denim shorts complete her outfit, showing more skin than I've seen on her before. I don't hide my obvious perusal of her and as my eyes make their way back up to her face, the most stunning smile greets me.

She hops into the car next to me and buckles up her seat belt. As soon as JP pulls away from her house, my hand can't control itself, her magnetism drawing me to her again. I rest my hand by her bare thigh and start running my index finger up and down the side of it, needing to feel her skin immediately. I can't help but peer into her eyes to gauge her reaction to me. I see my touch is, more than likely, responsible for the pink tinge now showing on her cheeks. Feeling brave, I slide my whole hand over her slim thigh, resting my fingers on her inner thigh above her knee, stroking her soft skin with my thumb. I get rewarded for my bravery with goose bumps setting her skin alight. I love knowing I affect her as much as she affects me. With identical grins on our faces, we both audibly sigh making us laugh out loud.

Arriving at school, we meet up with Rafe and Scott in the car park. As a group we walk to the school hall. They have both opted to wear shorts and t-shirts, feeling the heat like I am. Our whole student year is gathered, waiting to be split into groups. We all get handed a coloured shape. It symbolises the main group we will be in for the day. There's going to be two groups at each activity so we get to mix with different people throughout the day. I get a blue circle, the same as Rafe, so I give him a high five. JP gets a yellow triangle. And Scott and Tamsyn, to my annoyance, both get a purple square which means they will spend the whole day together. I will be lucky if I get one activity with her. We have to pin the shape to our tops so we can be identified easier.

The activities are being held at a retreat centre, down the road from our school so we all walk with our friends to start the day. You can sense the excitement from everyone in the air. I stay close to Tamsyn, needing to soak up as much of her as I can before she disappears for the day. I want to take her hand in mine, needing physical contact before she goes. Unfortunately, I don't know if she would appreciate me being so obvious with my affection in front of everyone. We are friends but there's something more to it, though either one of us is willing or brave enough to take the next step. At least Blake has been removed from the equation. One less thing for me to worry about.

As we arrive at the centre, we are welcomed by two rows of activity supervisors with their hands out, ready to give us high fives as we walk through their human tunnel. It has everyone in high spirits. We listen to the person in charge who explains how the day will go. We will move around to the different activities with one supervisor assigned to each group so we know where to go. We all go our separate ways as none of our shapes have been paired up for the first activity. Me and Rafe follow behind the rest of our group to a wide open hall with carpeted floors. A lady comes in, introducing herself as Hazel. She is going to take us through a meditation ritual. I scan the room and notice some of the students have blue circles like me and others have yellow circles. We are instructed to get comfy any way we desire. Me and Rafe try to hide our chuckles, finding it a bit hippy to start the day with. I decide to lie face down and rest my head on my arms. This way, I can hide my face if I find her airy fairy talk a bit too much to take. Rafe, on the other hand lies down with his limbs all outstretched from his body, facing up towards the ceiling. He's taking the bit about getting comfortable to a whole other level.

Hazel begins by telling us, "Breathe in and breathe out. Focus on your breathing. Be aware of your inhale and exhale. Slow it down. Breathe in deeply, filling your lungs with positive thoughts and holding for five, four, three, two, one and exhale breathing out all negativity and pushing it away from you." I focus on her voice, letting myself relax as I do. Letting her words sink in to me.

"Let your thoughts come to you and acknowledge them. Don't try to stop them. Let them come and go as they do. Just be aware. Focus on your breathing," she continues, in her light, flowing voice which has me sinking into a trance. Thoughts pass through my head; thoughts of school, thoughts of the guys and of my parents, thoughts of Blake's bloody face and finally of Tamsyn. I let all the other thoughts go and hold on to the ones of Tamsyn. My soul is fighting my mind to keep her in my thoughts longer. As I hold a thought of Tamsyn in my mind, more come to join her; her in the green dress, her under the shower, her walking out of her house this morning. They are all different facets of the girl, who has unknowingly stolen my heart.

I let the thoughts of her drift away from me, as Hazel's voice cuts through, "Imagine a meadow, the green grass underneath you. You are watching the clouds, taking in the day. The wind is whistling around you. Breathe in the fresh air. Breathe out any negativity you still hold and relax." I follow her voice paying attention, until I feel a sudden shake on my shoulder.

"Dude, wake up," Rafe says, waking me from my sleep. I must have dozed off during the meditation. I raise my sleepy eyes to an amused Rafe who's laughing.

"I can't believe you fell asleep," he says. "Come on, our group is moving on to the next activity." I push up off the floor with my hands, and then lightly punch Rafe on the shoulder returning his smile.

Our next activity is the trust fall and we are paired up with JP's group. His smile alone tells us he's happy to see us. He's got his friend Elijah in his group so at least he's not alone. There's a small structure they've made for us to fall off. The instructor informs us to bunch in close, in two lines with a couple people at the end. The rest of the group all line up, ready to let themselves fall into our waiting hands. Rafe is the first to take the leap into our arms. He turns around with no fear, knowing we will catch him and falls backwards off the structure. We all take his weight easily, catching him effortlessly. The group goes through, one at a time and then we switch. When it comes to my turn, I turn my back on the crowd below and breathe. Bracing myself for the fall, I tense and lean back. There's a moment of free falling before I hit their out spread arms. A smile creeps up my face, the fall is exhilarating.

After both groups have had turns, it's time to move onto our next activity. We have orienteering next while JP has meditation. After orienteering, we have an activity called 'alliteration names'. Someone in the group has to come up with a word with the same letter as our name to describe us. I get deemed as 'Tender Tate' by Rafe and someone calls out 'Rambunctious Rafe'. I do hear a girl nearby whisper, 'Raunchy Rafe,' as well which has me in hysterics.

This day has been the best day I've had in a long time. The day is flying by because when the activity is finished, we get led to a dining hall for lunch. We can mingle in here as all the groups are having lunch at the same time. My eyes, of their own accord, search for Tamsyn. There's four long rows of tables, from one end of the room to the other, with bench seats so everyone squeezes in next to one another. I find her seated along the far wall, laughing freely at something Scott said. JP is sitting on her other side. Me and Rafe fill up our plates with food and join them. They see us coming and Tamsyn smiles brightly at me. She must be enjoying the day as much as I am. Scott shuffles across, letting me squeeze in next to her and I give him a nod of thanks.

"What were you guys laughing about?" Rafe asks, wanting in on their joke.

"Have you guys had the free fall activity yet?" Scott asks us and we nod. "Well we got paired up with Blake and Leyla's group," he tells us. I turn to Tamsyn and she's trying to hold in her laughter. "Blake went up for his turn and at the last second most of us pulled our arms away, so he hit the ground hard," he says, cracking up with laughter and Tamsyn joins him. "Then Leyla refused to participate because she didn't want to risk getting dropped too. So they both sat to the side, with sulking expressions the whole time," which makes him and Tamsyn laugh harder. "So it's not only us pissed at those two. At least half of the students from our year are mad about how they treated T here," he says, smiling down the table at her fondly.

Jealousy spikes through me again. They are getting close. I wonder if she likes him better than me. I wouldn't blame her, he's a great guy. I'm a mess inside. I'm good at hiding it but it's still there. Can she see the ugliness threatening to spill out? Lost in my self-loathing, it takes me a minute to notice the soft, subtle touch on my thigh. I lower my hand under the table, to see what it is and my hand connects with her upwards facing palm. I thread my fingers into hers and she squeezes me tightly, making my thoughts settle down. Her touch calming me like nothing else does. I want to drag her hand to my lips and deliver a kiss there, showing her how much her gesture means to me. I'm not brave enough though. The guys all start talking and filling each other in on the activities they've had, when a small voice in the back of my head says, 'fuck it'. Still clutching her hand in mine, I turn my head her way leaning down towards her ear and breathe deeply of her scent, erasing my worries.

"I've missed you," I whisper to her, then deliver a kiss swiftly to the back of her ear. I have to restrain myself from nibbling her neck like a vampire. I sit back up straight taking her lingering scent with me. I peek over at her and she mouths the word, 'same,' at me, making my heart sing. We eat the rest of our lunch, secretly clutching hands under the table, while we listen to our friend's stories about their day.

We pack up our trays when we get instructed lunch is finished. Everyone is revitalised and ready to continue on with their day. Saying goodbye to the others, me and Rafe head over to our group leader, who has us follow her outside to a grassy area. A cloud of despair creeps in at the separation from Tamsyn after such a short time together. Luck must be on my side though, because for this activity, we are working with Tamsyn's group. Before I can get to her, the group instructor tells us about our activity. It's called 'The human knot.' She has us all stand in a circle and close our eyes. While we stand still, she moves people so we don't know where anyone is. Then she tells us, on the count of three, we are to move our hands forward to the middle of the circle and to find a hand to hold and not let go.

"One, two, three, go," she says, and everyone rushes forward. I have one thought in mind. Find the hand I know. The one I want to hold. Someone grasps my hand but they're hand is too big so I wriggle out of their grip. Another hand tries to grab me but it's too rough. Where is she? I hope someone hasn't already got her hands. In one last attempt to find her, I grasp another hand and I know immediately it's her. I intertwine our fingers and rub my thumb back and forth over my little spot on her hand. She rewards me with a squeeze. Jackpot! I knew it was her. It would have been embarrassing if it wasn't. I let my left hand grasp the next hand it finds. It's out of place in my hand though.

"Now open your eyes and without letting go of the hands you're holding, you have to untangle yourselves and form a circle again." I open my eyes and tug her hand to find out where she is. I'm rewarded with such a big smile, her eyes crinkling at the edges. Her smile alone has made this day perfect.

Everyone's pulling and trying to maneuver themselves out of the knot. Someone keeps pulling my left hand, trying to make me move but I'm too entranced with Tamsyn. I'm happy to spend the rest of the day standing here holding her hand so I don't try at all to make our way out of the knot.

"Tate," I hear from my side, so I let my eyes drop from Tamsyn and follow the voice calling my name. It's Scott. A finger tickles the middle of my other hand so I turn to him with a raised brow.

"Yes, it's me, you egg," he says laughing, as I've been ignoring him pulling on my hand for a while. Scott takes control of the situation because we need a leader if we are going to get out of this. He has people weaving over arms and twisting and turning. Freeing some, while others stay thoroughly tangled. Tamsyn has to climb over her other hand and then twists going under our joined hands. This movement brings her body flush up against me.

Scott the sneaky bastard says, "Tate, we will leave you like that for a bit and come back to you. Dante, move under Emma's hand there," giving me a covert wink. So here I stand, with Tamsyn pressed right up against me. Not able or willing to move away. I take a deep inhale as I gaze into her eyes. Her cheeks redden as she knows exactly what I'm doing. I'm addicted to her scent. I can't help it now. She's gotten under my skin.

I don't think Scott is trying to untangle anyone now. It's more like he's deliberately causing a bigger jumbled mess so me and Tamsyn can have this time together, without anyone thinking anything of it. It's not long before Rafe catches on to Scott's sneaky plan and he joins in. He's causing a loud ruckus trying to twist and turn, gaining everyone's attention. It gives me a cheeky moment to lean down and kiss Tamsyn on the forehead. I thought my nose was bad but now my lips can't stay away from her either. All too soon and the time for the activity is up. Both reluctant, we wait until the last possible second to let go and move a step back from each other. I give her a sad smile as my group goes one way and hers goes the other.

Next up we have 'Team seek and find.' We have a list of items we have to check off, matching with a different person in the group for each answer. We had to find someone born in the same month as us, someone who had a pet, someone who plays an instrument and so on. It was fun getting to know new things about some of my classmates.

Our next activity is 'Run free'. Our leader makes us wait a bit for the group joining us as they are running behind schedule. It doesn't bother me because I see Tamsyn and her group walk towards us. My whole body hums with excitement from being near her again. Our group leader explains the activity, saying one person is to be blindfolded while their partner leads them from a walk, to a jog to a full out run all while holding hands. I try to move closer to Tamsyn but our leader partners people up and puts Rafe with her instead. I get put with another girl from Tamsyn's group I don't know.

As we are walking out to the field we are going to do the activity in, Rafe drifts back to me and says to the girl who's my partner, "Kayla, do you want me to be my partner instead?" while putting on the charm. She falls for it, hook, line and sinker, jumping at the chance to be his partner. I fist bump him with a huge smile on my face and propel myself to the front of the group to tell Tamsyn I'm her new partner.

———————————————— **Tamsyn** ————————————————

I think my hormones are in overdrive today or else my nerve endings are going haywire every time Tate is close. His touch is electric; his hands send a shock straight through me every time there's contact between us. I wish I had gotten partnered with Tate but feel lucky considering I got Rafe, instead of someone I don't usually hang out with.

I'm daydreaming about Tate's green eyes and forcing myself not to turn around so I can catch a glimpse of them, when I hear a small, "Hey," come from the side of me. I slowly lift my gaze up and there are the green eyes I was trying so hard not to search for. They have come searching for me instead.

"Hey," I reply. I want to take his hand in mine; everything's better when he holds it. But I don't dare do it in front of everyone. I don't want everyone whispering about us.

"I'm your new partner," he tells me, and my face breaks out in a huge grin.

"Is that so?" I tease. "Is this your doing or Rafe's?" I ask.

"Rafe's but he did it for my benefit," he says so honestly. It's as if he wants me to know his feelings for me without him saying anything.

As we arrive at the field, their team leader hands out a blind fold to each pair.

"Do you want to get blind folded first or second?" he asks me.

"It doesn't bother me. I can go first," I say, so he tells me to turn around so he can tie the blind fold around me. As he lifts the blind fold up to cover my eyes, he steps forward into my back so he's pressed up firmly against me. With my sight gone, all my other senses are on high alert and all they are alerting me of is Tate. He knots the back of the blind fold tightly behind my head then runs his hands slowly down my arms, sending goose bumps over my skin. He grabs my hand and intertwines our fingers. He does his signature move of running his thumb back and forth causing more goose bumps to spring up which make him chuckle. He leans closer to me and as I breathe in his earthy scent, it overwhelms me. My lungs crave more of him so I take a deeper breath.

"If I didn't know any better, I'd say I have quite the effect on you Sweetness," he whispers softly into my ear. My cheeks heat up because he knows exactly what to do to get a reaction out of me.

"Okay teams. Off you go, whenever you're ready," the team leader says, and Tate gently leads me. I take tentative steps at first getting into a rhythm which is hard when I have to put all my trust in him. I know he will keep me safe; it's still unnerving when you can't see where you are walking.

"What's your favourite colour?" he randomly asks.

"Green," I reply, thrown by his question. "Yours?" I return.

"Red," he says.

"What about favourite food?" he tries another question.

"Hmm I love ice cream. And yours?" I counter.

"Anything but I do love pizza," he says.

"What's with all the questions?" I ask him. He stops walking so I stop next to him. He turns me so I'm facing him, still blindfolded, with his hands resting on my shoulders.

"I know when you're sad. I can see it written on your face without you having to say a word," he says softly to me letting the words sink in. I gulp and he moves a hand to cup my face rubbing his thumb over my cheek bone. "I know if I hold your face like this, you'll lean into my hand because you crave my touch, as much as I crave yours." And without me realising, I'm already leaning into his touch as he predicted. He lets go of my face, moving his hand back down to hold my hand. "I know your hands. I don't need to see them. I know them by feel now. I knew it was your hand, the second I touched you, back at the human knot activity. I know your scent as soon as I get a whiff of it in my direction. It draws me in. And lastly, I know your heart. Your heart is broken and damaged and you don't think you'll ever be able to fix it. I know this, because mine is exactly the same. Our hearts cried out to each other and I think it's why we have this special connection." My heart is about to leap out of my chest. He's saying all this and I still can't see him. It must be what is making him so brave. "We both need to heal Sweetness. You've had a full-on week but I want you to know, I'm here and when the right time comes, I'll still be here. So best friends are what we will be, right?" I can hear the smirk in his voice, replaying my words back to me.

"Yes, the best of friends," I tell him, with a smile.

"Well, best friends know the little things about each other, not only the big things. It's why I'm asking you all these questions. Ask your own questions too." He leans down and delivers a kiss to my forehead, which I must say is fast becoming my favourite spot he kisses. It makes me feel safe and no matter what is going on at the time, the moment he does it, I can breathe.

"Come on, let's run," he says with a chuckle, jerking me into a run and we laugh together as I follow wherever he leads me. My heart is freer than it has been in a long time.

Our last activity for the day involves all the groups gathering together in the dining hall. We are making a memory wall. We are to write or draw something from today or something meaningful to us. There's paper, paints, crayons and coloured pencils littered all over the tables so everyone finds a spot and gets to work. I'm already with Tate, Scott and Rafe so we find JP who's sitting where we were for lunch and take a seat. I know exactly what I want to draw; Tate's star. But I want to draw the one letting the light in because I want to start doing that now. So I grab a thick black crayon, a piece of paper and create my artwork. So enthralled by my drawing, I don't notice much else going on around me. It isn't until I feel Tate's hand on my thigh under the table, I come back to reality. I'm about to lower my hand under the table to hold his but he leans in towards me.

"Carry on, you're enjoying yourself. I couldn't help myself, I needed your touch. I can work with one hand," he tells me quietly, so only I can hear him. I give a slight nod to acknowledge what he said, not wanting to draw attention. Now he's distracting me by drawing circles with his finger on my thigh. I try not to giggle and focus on my star.

"Everyone, once you've finished your artwork come up and pin it on the wall please," one of the team leaders instructs us. I'm nearly finished so I tell Tate I'm going to go pin mine up. I wander up to the wall and grab a push pin. I press the little pin through my paper into the wall, holding it in place. Taking a step back, I admire my star. It looks good up there. While I'm appreciating my work, Tate comes up and pins his right next to mine and steps back for me to see. It's a simple rainbow.

I turn to him smiling, and he leans down and whispers, "There's always a rainbow after a storm." My eyes glaze over with unshed tears because, once again, he's directed his kindness at me, without me asking.

"Thank you," is all I can say to him. He leads me back to our seats and the guys take turns going up to the wall as they finish their pieces.

After everyone has put a piece on the wall, we all stand up, make a semicircle and admire everyone's work. My eyes zone in on the dark star with the rainbow close by. We are given another five minutes to stand there and reflect on the day we've had. I must say it's been a great day. I've laughed a lot and enjoyed myself, more than I have in a long time.

"Thank you everyone for the amazing work you put into this day and for making it so enjoyable. I hope you can take something away with you today. Now, your teachers have told me if you'd like to leave here and go home, you are more than welcome or else you can walk back to school and go home from there," the event leader tells us.

Everyone, with excitement in the air, rushes out of the dining hall, taking off in different directions. Me and the guys start walking back to school because it's where JP's car is. We are all on a high from the days' events. It's been a long day though and my feet are starting to hurt, from being on them most of the time. Tate must notice, as he bends down in front of me.

"Jump on my back, Sweetness. I'll give you a piggyback ride." I giggle, as I climb onto his back wrapping my arms around his neck tightly and he holds my legs firmly in place, with his hands on my thighs.

"Wow, you are so tall. I can see everything from up here," I tell him, and the guys hear and start laughing. I am teeny next to all of them so what do they expect? Tate's gait slows a bit and we drop behind the others who are laughing and joking around, as we walk the way we came back to school.

"Did you have a good day?" he asks me.

"Yes, I did. Did you?"

"The best," he says, with a squeeze of my thighs. Feeling brave, I give him a hug from the back, tightening my hold around his neck. Leaning to the side, I give him a quick kiss to the temple.

"What was that for?" he asks, with a smile in his voice.

"For being you," I say, as a way of explanation. Satisfied with my answer, he doesn't ask me to explain further.

He carries me all the way to school and doesn't put me on my feet until we are right beside the car. We all pile in, taking the seats we did yesterday. I can't help but snuggle into Tate and shut my eyes, enjoying this moment for a minute before I have to get out. Scott gets dropped off first then in no time at all, JP is pulling up in front of my house.

"I'll see you guys on Monday," I tell them, as I hop out of the car, smiling at Tate as I turn my back on him and walk up the path.

"Check your pocket," he yells, as they pull away and drive off, but not before I notice the huge smile plastered on his face. With a goofy grin on my face, I check my pockets and feel a piece of paper in one so I pull it out. I unfold the white piece of paper, and there written in colourful rainbow writing are the letters 'BFF' and I can't help the warmth, spreading from my heart and taking over my whole body.

Tamsyn

It's Saturday night. I worked on school assignments all day and now my brain is ready for sleep. It's late as I tried to mentally drain myself so I could sleep without any dreams but it hasn't happened. I've been lying here in the dark, for who knows how long, with my brain running riot on me. At this rate I don't think I'll get any sleep.

A 'DING' comes from my bedside table. As I grab my phone, I glance at the clock and see its nearly midnight. Opening the text message, I see it's from Tate and a smile ignites on my face filling my stomach with butterflies.

T: You awake?

S: Yeah, I am. How come you are still up?

T: Can't sleep. What about you?

S: Same.

T: Want to sneak out and come for a walk with me?

The butterflies take flight at the prospect of seeing Tate tonight.

S: Yes.

T: Good because I'm already outside your house so get your sweet butt down here.

Oh my goodness. He's already here. I quietly step to my closet and throw on baggy track pants and a hoodie and slip on my trainers. I sneakily open my door, hoping it doesn't make a sound and alert my mum. Stealthily, I creep down the stairs to the front door, turning the handle before opening it. I creep out onto the dark porch and slowly close it trying not to make a sound. A soft click lets me know it's shut. I'm about to search for Tate, when warm arms wrap around my waist and lift my feet off the porch. I yelp in surprise.

"Sshh or your mum will hear you and all your secret ninja skills were put to use for nothing," he whispers in my ear, his warm breath tickling my face. He swings me around in his arms. My legs and arms unconsciously wrap around him as he jogs away from my house, holding onto me tightly. He continues until he's a few houses away then peeks at me and slows his pace. Lowering the hoodie from my head, he brushes the hair from my face.

"There. We should be out of earshot now," he says, dropping me to my feet.

"So, what has you walking the streets in the middle of the night?" I ask him, as we walk side by side.

"I couldn't get to sleep. So sometimes I go for a run and my feet ended up bringing me here. I texted you on the off chance you might be up. I thought some quality time with my best friend was called for," he says, with a smirk giving me a nudge with his arm. "How come you were awake?" he asks me back.

"Same, I guess. I couldn't get to sleep, my mind wouldn't shut off," I confess.

"Two peas in a pod," he says, smiling and it has the butterflies circling. "So best friend of mine, how about we keep getting to know each other? Do you have a favourite animal?"

"Pig for sure. They're so damn cute. And I don't eat pork, ham or bacon because of them," I tell him truthfully, not caring what he will think. He has that effect on me. I could tell him anything and he wouldn't judge me. He lets out a slight chuckle. "It shows huge dedication to your favourite animal, I must say," he tells me, with amusement clear on his face.

"What's yours then?" I ask, trying to get the attention off me.

"Hmm, I think it would have to be an elephant. They are extremely majestic plus I've always wanted to ride one," he tells me.

"Okay, my question. If you could be a girl for a day, what would you want to do?" I ask, trying not to giggle. He lets a boisterous laugh take over.

He thinks for a moment before replying, "Good question. I want to know why girls go to the bathroom in groups so it would be my top priority. But please, make it a day when I don't get my period. Not something I would not like to experience." We both burst into a fit of laughter as we walk down the quiet street, sounds of our cheerfulness blown away with the wind.

"Oh my goodness, I can't believe you said that," I chuckle, while swatting at his chest.

"What would you do if you were a boy for a day?" he says, countering my question.

"I would try peeing, standing up. Guys may look at me weird though because it will be spraying everywhere since I won't know what I'm doing." We both crack up with laughter again.

As we are walking the streets under the star covered sky, I smile to myself thinking this boy has changed my life in such a short amount of time. A stranger at first and now he's become the most important person to me. All from seeing what no one else bothered to notice; Me. He's a couple steps ahead of me then suddenly stops. Pivoting around with the biggest grin on his face, he takes my hand and tugs me while he jogs forward.

"What is it?" I ask amused, as it must be something good to make him smile like that. In no time at all, we are standing in front of a taped off piece of concrete on the footpath.

"They must have put this down today, it's still wet," he says, while bending down to poke it with his finger. "We need a stick," he decides and searches around for one.

"What are you going to do with a stick?" I ask him. He stops his scouring to give me the most mischievous grin. Oh no, this can't be good. He spots a scraggly twig sticking out of a nearby gutter and picks it up.

He crouches down, "Sweetness, can you hold the tape up while I do this quickly?" he asks me. Intrigued by what he's going to do, I oblige standing beside his crouched form watching him. He leans forward balancing on the balls of his feet and writes something with his stick. It doesn't take long and then he's standing next to me. I drop the tape I was holding and both of us gaze down at the imperfect concrete. 'TNT' he's written.

"Tate and Tamsyn," he says proudly. "It will be our little secret," he smugly says. The butterflies are whirling around taking flight in my belly while we stand there, staring in silence at the now more beautiful concrete. I thread my fingers through his, holding onto this boy who has become my best friend.

We carry on with our midnight adventure, walking hand in hand with no destination in mind. Walking and listening to the sounds of our footsteps thudding on the footpath, neither of us talking, letting the calm silence surround us. We embrace the quiet, not needing words to fill the void. Up ahead, I notice a kid's playground so I tug Tate towards the swings.

"Push me please," I say, as I grab the chains and wriggle myself into the seat. His large hands push against my lower back and I'm moving forward. Kicking my legs, I pick up momentum so the swing can take me into the sky. My hair whips around my face, the higher I go. Tate takes a seat on the other empty swing next to me and soon he is joining me, soaring through the air. Closing my eyes, I breathe. My body slices back and forth through the still night, feeling free for a moment. My mind has pushed everything away and for this small moment in time, I just am. No heartache, no grief, no fear. I'm just me.

We stay for a while, swinging in the darkness. The smallest light source, coming from the full moon shining brightly above us. I hear Tate's soft laughter drift into my ear and turn to him. A smile etched on his face. Something's different now, he appears less bogged down as if a weight has been lifted off him for a minute. Is he as sad as I am sometimes? I never asked him about what's going on with him. Trying to hide my own issues has me not seeking his issues out either. But I should. Not today though. Today I will let us be happy; happy in this moment. Happy and free.

"If you could have one superpower, what would it be and why?" he calls to me, through the darkness, as we rock back and forth.

"I think being able to fly would be a cool one. I am so free now. Imagine feeling this way all the time?" I say, and he nods with a small tug on his lips agreeing.

"What about you?" I ask him.

Without hesitation he says, "The ability to heal. If I could heal people of everything, I would. I would take away their injuries and diseases and relieve them of their pain and suffering. It would make the world a better place. How it was meant to be. You know?" I nod, because it sounds like a cool ability to have. Then I could heal myself and wouldn't have to suffer any more. His answer is so deep and meaningful. It makes me wonder who he wants to heal so badly. Me, himself or is he talking about someone else?

A yawn escapes my mouth, and I try to hide it behind my hand but Tate has already seen it.

"Come on, let's get you back home before your mum realises you're missing," he says, then he jumps off his swing landing on his feet. He turns around smiling at me.

"Show off," I say, as I slow my swing down and hop off once it's stopped.

"Jump on, I'll give you a piggyback ride home," he says, bending down to let me climb on his back. I walk up behind him, wrap my arms around his neck and he stands up effortlessly as if I'm no burden to carry at all. He hooks his hands around my legs, holding them against his waist. I snuggle my face into the side of his neck, inhaling him, letting his earthy scent, calm my soul. He always smells so good.

It's peaceful being out at night with no one else around, like we are the only two people in the world. Before I know it, we are standing on the path leading to my house.

"Home sweet home," Tate whispers, in case my mum hears us out here.

"Thanks for tonight, I needed that," I tell him, as we walk quietly up the path to the porch. I climb a couple of steps, while Tate stays on the path below making us more equal in height.

"Thank you for coming with me, Sweetness. Now go get some sleep. I don't want my best friend to be tired now," he says, with humour in his voice.

"Goodnight Tate," I say with a big smile. He reaches up, brushing the hair from my face and tucks it behind my ear. Staring into my eyes he leans in, it has me holding my breath. Our faces are so close, if I lean an inch forward I could touch his lips but I choose to hold still. My eyes close of their own accord and I feel the gentlest kiss on the side of my mouth. If it was a fraction to the left, he would have got my lips. It burns my skin as he pulls away. I open my eyes and he's watching me, while taking visible deep breaths.

"Goodnight Sweetness," he whispers as he steps back. I back up too until I hit the door, opening it quietly and I sneak back inside seeing him run away from my house. I lean against the closed door after I shut it. Taking deep breaths myself, I bring my fingers up and caress where his lips touched. Still able to feel his lingering kiss, long after he's gone. Too absorbed in my thoughts, it doesn't register he was running in the opposite direction of his house.

_______________________________Tate_____________________________

Sprinting away into the night, I need to burn off this energy or else I'll never get to sleep. My body is humming with the need to take her in my arms. I was so close to kissing her. My lips desperately needed to touch her, and my mind directed them to the side of her mouth at the last second. I can't help myself when I'm around her. She draws me in and I lose all sense of myself. She takes over my mind so all my thoughts are consumed with her.

Once she is out of sight, my mind becomes cleared of her and I'm tormented by my thoughts. All the thoughts she subdues, come pounding back in like a freight train, overwhelming me and tearing me down again. I can't keep going on like this. She's been the perfect distraction but I fear her power over me won't last. Soon I'll be surrounded by my guilt she triggers. How long can I go on trying to save her, without saving myself? For a second, I let my hurt out of its cage. I let her image come to the forefront of my mind. Long, blonde hair sweeps down her face to her shoulders. Sparkling green eyes, exactly like mine, stare back at me. Stare into me. Quinn.

I take a deep breath in and as I exhale, I push the image back in its cage, where it must stay to keep me safe. It threatens to unlock so I push myself faster and harder. Pummeling the concrete with my strides,

I run as fast as I can, leaving all of me behind, punishing myself until I'm numb again. Only then will I be able to sleep. Free from pain, free from hurt, free from myself.

Chapter 17
~

________________________Tate________________________

The week begins pretty uneventfully but on Tuesday morning, I have another set back. Driving to school with JP and Tamsyn has become our new routine.

While entranced with Tamsyn, like I usually am these days, her face lights up and she says, "JP, can you turn the music up please? It's my favourite song." He obliges and the upbeat music blasts through the car, causing my heart to pound in my chest. Tamsyn happily sings along to the lyrics, unaware of the feelings they stir inside me.

Her face morphs, into the blonde girl with the sparkling green eyes, facing me with a cheeky grin on her face, while she continues singing. I squeeze my burning eyes shut, trying to rid myself of the memory. My heart is hammering away in my chest as the music screams in my ears. I feel a touch on my leg and my eyes fly open at the contact and stare at her. The blonde girl has gone. The brown haired girl in her place.

"JP, turn it down," she yells over the music, so she can be heard. When the music quietens, she tries to connect with me.

"Tate, are you okay?" I unbuckle and push myself to the other side of the car, needing space from her. I can sense the tears pricking the back of my eyes, searching for release.

"Tate?" she tries again. I can feel the all too familiar increase of my breaths and I know I need to get away from her. This girl who I long for, but who also makes my heart ache, and not in a good way.

"Don't," I plead, as I keep my distance. I rub my chest with the heel of my hand, hoping it will ease the pain. The car stops and I see we are at a red light. My first thought is survival. To survive, I need to get away from the thing causing my pain, which at this moment is Tamsyn. She makes me feel too much without doing anything. I fumble to open the door and scramble to the footpath, and then out of habit, my feet accelerate taking me away, keeping me safe. How can I save her from drowning when she pulls me under my own wave, without realising what she is doing?

My feet carry me home and I release all the pain, once I'm in my room. It takes longer than usual to calm my breaths, and my face is soaked with tears by the time I settle. Sitting on the floor against my bed, I stare at the wall, not able to cope but needing to survive.

JP bangs on my door later on in the day. I don't know how many hours have passed.

"Come in," I croak out. He steps into my room and I instantly know there's pity, streaked across his face.

"You okay, bro? You missed the whole day at school," he asks, worry laces his voice.

"Yeah, I am now," I tell him. I take a breath and then ask, "Is Tamsyn alright?"

"She was shaken up by you taking off but I told her to give you some space and you would be okay," he explains.

"Thanks man," I say, thankful I have JP to help me through this.

He lets out a sigh before he says, "I don't want you getting angry at me but I need to say this. One of you is going to end up hurt. At first, I thought it was going to be you but now I'm not so sure bro. Tamsyn is fragile and I can tell she triggers you. Maybe your friendship isn't the best thing right now. I'm worried about both of you."

"I can handle it man. Drop it," I tell him, anger starting to fill my veins. He walks to the door and leaves without another word. I can handle it, can't I?

Tamsyn gives me space and acts like nothing happened the next day. Ms. Chadwick informs us we need to bring a white singlet, if possible, and some shorts to class on Friday. It's a way for us to learn the muscles we have been learning this week. Tamsyn has gone back into her shell again. Sometimes she pops out and I get glimpses of the girl I know is in there. However, the majority of the time, the girl I know is so pummeled down by the shadows plaguing her, she can't see the light. Who am I to judge? I'm no better than her. I'm better at pretending than she is. She doesn't hide her pain now, she wears it on her face, clearly for anyone who knows her to see. I hope I'm not the cause of any of her shadows. I can usually keep my pain hidden well. It's how I function. If I let it show, I will break. And those pieces won't ever go back together. How could they? The biggest piece of all is missing.

——————————————— Tamsyn ———————————————

It's Friday and the last period of the day. Human bio. I haven't mentioned Tate's breakdown in the car the other day. I hoped he would open up to me but I don't think that will happen. He's gone back to pretending like everything is fine with him.

I enter the room with Tate and the guys when I hear Ms. Chadwick addressing the class, "Could everyone make their way to the bathrooms to get changed. I'll give you a few minutes then we are going to start work on a revision technique, to help you learn and remember the muscles of the body." Everyone wanders off, boys and girls going in different directions.

I enter the bathroom and go into a stall, placing my bag on the hook. I unzip my backpack and find the clothes I'd packed in there this morning. I grab the hem of my uniform top and pull it over my head, place it in my bag and take out my white singlet. I examine my bra. At least it's my pretty, purple one I wore today. I didn't think about it when I grabbed my see-through singlet this morning. I guess I can't do much about it now. I put my arms into the holes and pull it over my head, tugging my hair out from the back of it. I unzip my skirt and unhook the safety pin I have secured at the side. I had to start using it when my skirt started sliding off, even when zipped up. I could probably benefit from eating more. The fabric falls to the floor. Kicking it up into my hands, I place it in my bag and grab my shorts. I step out of my shoes, as my tight, black bike shorts will be too hard to get on over them. I place my feet through the holes and yank the shorts up my legs. Bending down, I squeeze my feet back into my shoes without undoing the laces. I zip up my bag, throw it over my shoulder and unlock the stall. A lot of the other girls from class are happily getting changed in front of the mirror, not caring for privacy like I did. Most of them, checking their reflections and touching up their makeup.

I wander back to class and most of the guys are already at their seats changed. It didn't take them long to get changed. I squeeze into my seat between Tate and Scott, watching Tate out of the corner of my eye. Everyone was required to wear a white singlet so we could write over it, if we wished. Tate's singlet clings to his torso like a second skin. His thick arms are defined but not overly like Rafe's are, from hitting the gym too much. Tate's is more natural. He's muscular without trying. It's his natural physique.

For once I don't lie my head down on the desk, I'm interested in this lesson. I will never admit it out loud, but I'm especially interested in catching glimpses of Tate's muscles. All the girls finally return to class and take their seats. Some of them throw glances Tate's way, trying to check out his muscles. It sends a spike of protectiveness through me. I don't want them looking at him or fantasising about him. A few of them turn around in their seats, their gazes directed at Rafe, so I peek down the row at him and he's flexing his arms for the girls to ogle. He's such a flirt.

"Okay class," Ms. Chadwick says, breaking me away from my thoughts "I'm handing out a list of all the major muscles we are going over today. We will see how many we can get through. You can either cut these out or you can write directly on your partner, whichever you and your partner decide. Use your textbook. On the back page are the diagrams, you need to match up the muscles on your partner." Jeez, I'm going to have to interact with someone now. I hope I get partnered up with someone who knows what they're doing.

"I want you to partner up with the person seated next to you. Move into your own little space in the room and we can get started," Ms. Chadwick instructs. My eyes nearly bug out of my head or I think they do anyway, because it means my partner is Tate. We haven't acknowledged the other morning, so I'm hoping it won't be awkward. I feel self-conscious with my see through singlet on. Oh my gosh, is he going to stare at my bra now? I slowly lift my head to meet his gaze and he's staring down at me with the sweetest smile.

"Hi," is all he says, and it makes my lips curl up at him, calming me. "Are you going to be alright with me as your partner? It's not going to be awkward with me being a guy or anything?" He asks me. I observe my classmates in the room and note there are a few other mixed sex partners, not only us, so it makes me relax a bit more.

"No, it's fine Tate. If you're good to go, so am I," I say. No need to be awkward when he's my best friend right? He grabs the sheet with the names of the muscles typed on it.

"Do you want to cut these out or should we write on each other? Whatever you want to do, I'm happy with it," he says.

"We can write on each other's skin, if you don't mind having to wash it off later? It's the last period of the day so it's not like we'll have to walk around school all day with it on," I reply.

He chuckles, "Cool, let's do that." He grabs two markers off his desk and then leads me to the corner of the class, off to the side of our desks.

"So, where should we start?" he asks.

"Hmm well, we could either start head to toe or we could start from the top of the list, and work our way down if you like?" I suggest.

"Yeah, I like the idea of working from the list then we can see how many we know without peeking at the diagrams." I nod in agreement. It sounds like a good idea. "Let's take turns picking one and writing them on the other person. You can start if you like." He holds out the markers for me to choose one. I grab the black one because I figure it will be harder to wash off than the red. He runs his eyes through the list.

"Okay, so first on the list is Trapezius," he says. I've got no idea where that is. I'm now wishing I had paid more attention in this class so I don't appear dumb in front of him. "Come here and turn around, I need your back," he says while wiggling his finger in a 'come hither' motion at me. I take the last few steps towards him and turn around, so my back is to him. "The Trapezius is a large muscle on the upper back," he tells me "and it gets its name from its Trapezoidal shape. I'm going to touch you now," he informs me. He lightly grabs my ponytail and sweeps it to the side of my right shoulder, running his fingers softly over my skin as he does. Just breathe Tam, I tell myself, just breathe. He places his hand firmly on my left shoulder, and asks "Is it alright to draw on your singlet because I'm going to get the top of it?"

"Yeah, that's fine, go ahead," I reply. He places the marker at the base of my neck and draws a line down my neck and along the back of my shoulder. Then he moves diagonally to the middle of my upper back, dragging the marker towards my other shoulder and back to the starting point at my neck. He delicately writes Trapezius across my upper back, his feather light touch tickling wherever he touches.

"There, Trapezius," he says. I turn around to face him and he's smiling. "Your turn," he smirks at me.

"You better have written Trapezius on my back and not something embarrassing," I say. He laughs so loud, he draws a few looks from other students.

With a cheeky grin he says, "Well you will have to trust me, won't you?" I can't help but smile back at him, his mood is infectious. I break eye contact to see what's next on the list. Achilles tendon. Lucky, I know this one.

"Achilles," I say to him. I take my marker and bend down as he turns around to give me the back of his leg. I angle my head sideways, holding his leg while I write Achilles from his heel, upwards along the bottom of his leg. Writing over the hair on his legs is a bit hard but I get it done. I stand up and he turns his leg to examine my work. Smiling, he looks at the list scanning to see what he has next.

"Deltoid," he says, "do you know where it is?" I shake my head feeling like an idiot for not knowing. "It's the shoulder muscle," he tells me, as he quickly grabs my forearm and brings me closer to him. I look up at his green eyes as he stares down at me.

We gaze at each other until Ms. Chadwick's voice breaks our trance, "Good work everyone, keep going." He shakes his head gently and focusses on my shoulder. He lets go of my forearm and runs a finger up my arm to my shoulder, so slowly, it makes me tremble. I can tell he notices my shiver when his lips tease into the slightest smile, his eyes crinkling around the edges. You would think with the way he smiles, he enjoys teasing me with his touch, knowing how it affects me. He grabs my upper arm and bends his head to get closer to my shoulder. My breath catches so I turn my head away from him. The movement he made was feeling too intimate, especially while surrounded by our classmates. His marker softly glides against my skin as he writes and outlines the muscle. He releases his hold and I turn my neck to peer at his work.

"What's next on the list?" I ask him.

"Pectoralis, major and minor. I'm guessing for now we are classifying them together," he says. I give him a blank stare. I don't know where these muscles are either. Biting my lip, he must realise I'm a bit confused.

"Have you heard of pecs before?" he asks. Movement on his chest catches my eye, and he's raising his chest muscles one at a time and smirking at me. I can't help it, I burst out laughing, covering my mouth with my hand. His eyes soften and he pulls my hand away from my mouth.

"Don't hide your smile, please. It looks good on you," he says, making my cheeks heat.

"Class, we have about ten more minutes then we will start packing up. Finish off your last couple of muscles. Rafe, you didn't need to take your singlet off, you were supposed to write over it," Ms. Chadwick's voice breaks through our moment again. Rafe's response gets drowned out because I'm so focussed on Tate.

"Okay, so Pectoralis muscles are pecs," I say. His singlet dips a bit down his chest so I ask, "Do you want me to write over your singlet or under it?" His throat bobs as he visibly takes a big gulp.

Without breaking eye contact he softly says, "Under". His hand moves up and grabs the top of his singlet, pulling it down to bare his soft skin with defined muscle under it. I have to reach up on my tippy toes to write. Balancing myself by holding onto his arm, he helps steady me by gripping my upper arm. I keep my focus on his chest and quickly write the word pecs. Leaning back onto my heels, I take a step away from him. The energy surrounding us is electric. I haven't felt anything like this before; it's unnerving. He busies himself with the list, taking his time. Maybe he is as affected by me as I am by him.

"Quadriceps is next," he says. "Do you know which muscles they are?

"They're in the thigh right?" I question.

"Yeah it's the group of muscles in the front of the thigh and hamstrings are in the back," he tells me. "The bell is going to go soon so this will probably be our last one." He takes a step closer to me, and squats down to get better access to my thigh. "Umm Sweetness? Your shorts are going to have to get hiked up a bit so I can write."

My fingers grab the edges of my bike shorts on my right leg, and I roll it up as high as it can go.

"That will do," he tells me. Looking down at him, he's staring at me with those all-knowing forest green eyes, like he sees right into my soul. His hand softly slides up the back of my leg, starting at my ankle and making its way up to my thigh. He grips my thigh, making it easier for him to write. My breathing picks up from having his hand on me so I scan the room and settle on the clock to distract me while he writes, not being able to watch him while he's in front of me. Staring at the clock, I start counting the seconds until the bell goes. He is taking forever to write. His hand moves and he quickly rolls down my shorts and he bounces back up and stands.

"Done," he says, as the bell goes.

"Great work today class. I hope it has helped you. You can go home in your clothes, no need to get back into uniforms. Rafe, put your singlet on before you leave please. Enjoy your weekend everyone," Ms. Chadwick's voice booms over the bell.

I hand Tate back his black marker and quickly pack up my books into my bag. Tate quietly puts his things away too. Before I pull away from the desk, his voice stops me.

"Hey Tamsyn?" Tate says. My eyes question him, not sure what he's about to say. "Enjoy your weekend scrubbing the marker off," he chuckles.

Smirking, I reply, "I think you'll have a worse time than me since the black marker said it was permanent." His smile instantly drops, and I can't help but laugh loudly as I walk away. I leave him in a frantic state, double checking to see if his marker was permanent. It isn't but the expression on his face is priceless.

Smiling to myself, I charge down the hallway, knowing it's a matter of time before Tate catches up with me once he figures out I was joking about the marker.

"You little liar," I hear a second Tate yell, before he grabs me and throws me with my bag over his shoulder. I'm laughing so hard now.

"Tate, put me down, this is embarrassing," I say into his back, as I try punching it hoping he will let me go. I don't think my punches are hard as he walks unaffected. So I give up, and give in to hanging there like a rag doll.

As we get outside, I see JP walking behind us to his car. Well I hear his cackling laughter, before I see him.

"What did you do Ice Queen, to get stuck up there?" he mocks me. His use of my nickname has me still for a moment, before my brain catches up, and I realise he's using it with affection now and not in a hateful way.

"I did nothing at all. Tate here, can't take a joke," I say, huffing from irritation at being stuck on his shoulder. To prove he's in control and I shouldn't complain, Tate uses his other hand to tickle my side, causing me to break into fits of uncontrollable laughter.

"I'm sorry. I'm sorry," I say between laughs. "Please, put me down now." He finally obliges and pulls my legs towards the ground, which has my whole body sliding down the front of his. When my face gets in line with his, he holds me there, as if I weigh nothing. Staring into my eyes, I see humour on his face. I want to wipe the smirk off his face so I wrap my legs around his waist, my arms wrapping around his neck and I bury my head into his neck. His arms automatically embrace me too, holding me tightly to him. With my head tucked away from view, I'm tempted to blow a raspberry on him but I choose to plant a gentle kiss on his neck instead, right where his pulse is. Lingering there, his pulse speeds up. Bingo! I pull my head up to look at his eyes and all humour has gone from his eyes, now replaced with want.

"See, I can play dirty too," I tell him, trying to keep a serious face but I end up laughing, which doesn't help when he tickles me again. By the time we get to the car JP, Rafe and Scott are already in their seats amused at our antics. I slide into the middle seat for a change and Tate climbs in next to me. All of my previous worries about it being awkward between us, drift away. After dropping Scott off, we pull up to my house and I get out.

"Sweetness?" Tate calls to me from the open window, and he has me turning back with raised brows. "Have a good weekend." I smile and nod as I walk up the path to my house. As the car pulls away, I realise it's the first Friday in a month he hasn't given me a note and my heart sinks a bit with disappointment. Those notes had been the bright spot of my week and I looked forward to them when I realised they were going to keep coming. I don't know why he does it on Fridays. Is it so he could leave me with something to get through the weekend. As I get to the front door of my house, I'm a bit disappointed I won't have a note to add to my collection.

"Hey Mum," I yell out, when I get inside the front door.

"Hi dear, I'm going out tonight to catch up with a friend. So I've left some money on the kitchen bench for you to order some dinner. I hope I've left enough," she says. Stopping on the bottom step, I turn to her and see she's dressed up which I haven't seen her do in a while.

"Wow, you look nice Mum. I can easily make myself something. I don't eat much these days anyway," I tell her.

"Umm about that dear," she says, biting her nails, "I rang the boys' mums today and they said it is fine for the boys to come spend the night here again with you. I will feel better about going out if I know you are taken care of at home," she says, staring at the ground and I know she's still worried about me. I guess I can't magically make her stop worrying, not after what I put her through the other night.

"Mum, what if the guys had plans? I don't need a babysitter," I try to argue.

"Please, don't make a big deal out of this Tamsyn. Their mums were going to send the boys right over, once they had a chance to get their stuff together. They should be here soon. So if you want to clean yourself up a bit before they come, you better hurry." She nudges me up the stairs.

I carry on up the stairs, dropping my bag by the door. Since I don't have a note from Tate, I choose to examine his writing on my skin instead before I wash it off. I better hurry before they arrive. Butterflies in my belly take flight at the fact I'll be seeing Tate again so soon. I stand in front of my floor length mirror and try angling myself to see my back, where he's written Trapezius. Luckily it was all he had written and didn't embarrass me. Next, I look at my shoulder to the word Deltoid delicately written. He has nice handwriting for a guy. I slide my fingers down into my bike shorts and tug them off, stepping out of them and then positioning myself back in front of the mirror.

"What the..?" I loudly whisper to myself, as I peer down at my thigh with the red writing across it, trying to make out what it says. It's a bit hard to read upside down so I read it through the mirror, it's backwards in the reflection. My eyes become misty as I read what Tate's written. It says, 'I see you and what I see is beautiful'. My shaking hand comes up to cover my silent cries. He didn't forget to write me a note. I wonder if he realises how special his notes have become for me. I'm still amazed this incredible boy sees me when no one else does. I grab my phone out of my bag and snap a photo of my leg, wanting to have proof of his note before I have to wash it off. Examining the picture, my heart warms at the fact he thinks I'm beautiful. He sees the beauty, through the mess, which is me.

_________________________________Tate_________________________________

When we get home from dropping Tamsyn off, I receive an unexpected but pleasant surprise. Mrs. Winter had called and spoken to my aunt, asking her if me and JP could go stay the night with Tamsyn. She wanted to go out with a friend but was a bit apprehensive to leave Tamsyn home alone, not knowing what state of mind she is in. I'm shocked my aunt willingly agreed since it caused such drama between us the last time we stayed at her house. I'm more than happy to stay with Tamsyn again so don't fight it when she says it's all sorted. JP surprisingly isn't too put out that his plans for Friday night are sorted for him. He flicks a text to Scott and Rafe to tell them what we are up to for the night. Funnily enough, Mrs. Winter has contacted their mums too, organising the same thing. So that's where I find myself now, sitting outside Scott's house waiting for him. We already picked up Rafe and once Scott gets here, we'll leave for Tamsyn's house. I wonder if she noticed the note I wrote on her leg. It took me longer than I thought it would, to rub the black marker off my skin. Luckily it wasn't permanent. My heart picks up speed at the thought of spending the night with Tamsyn. I'm lost in my thoughts as Scott comes bounding from his house.

"Slumber party time," he says cheerily, as he hops in the car.

"I'm surprised you guys are so easy going about this. I thought you'd want to go to some party tonight," I say to the guys.

"Tamsyn is one of us now dude, if she needs us, we will be there. Even if it includes us spending a Friday night in," Rafe says from his seat in the back. They all nod in agreement and I am lucky I found this group of friends.

Pulling up to Tamsyn's place we get out, lugging our bags up to her house. Rafe knocks on the door and Mrs. Winter lets us in.

"Thank you so much for coming. You are doing me a huge favour," she tells us gratefully.

"It's no problem at all Tanya. We're happy to help. Plus Tamsyn is our friend and we help our friends, when we can," JP tells her.

Smiling back at us, she says, "I've left some money on the bench for you and there's snacks in the cupboard because I know you will get hungry later."

"Thanks," we all say, in unison.

"Hey guys," we hear from behind us. Turning around, my heart catches. There stands Tamsyn with dripping, wet hair, hanging down her back. A baby blue tank top, clings to her skin and her matching sleep shorts are so short. I can't help gulp away the feelings they are igniting in me.

I must be staring because I hear, "Tate," come from her and I don't know how long I've stood there, gawking at her. It must have been a while as the boys snigger behind me. I look at Tamsyn and she's shyly smiling at me, pink glowing on her cheeks.

"Boys, you know where the mattresses are. How about you get started setting them up?" Tanya suggests, as it takes the attention away from my awkward moment of staring at Tamsyn. The guys race past her up the stairs to get the room sorted, while I stand there smiling at my best friend.

"Hey," I stupidly say, not knowing what else to say after she caught me staring red handed. I should ask her to put something else on, those shorts are far too distracting. Her mum leaves the room to give us a minute of privacy, which I appreciate. She skips down the last few steps to meet me at the bottom.

"Thanks for coming. I won't admit it to mum but I was a bit anxious when she said she was going out and I thought I would be home by myself," she tucks a piece of wet hair behind her ear as she talks. I take her hand in mine, bringing her frail hand to my lips and lay a gentle kiss on the back of her knuckles.

"It's our pleasure," I tell her, while keeping eye contact.

"Thanks for the note too," she says, lowering her eyes to the ground; I see the pink on her cheeks deepening to a red. Instinctively, I grab her chin and raise it gently, so I can look into her eyes.

"It's the truth," I tell her adamantly, hoping my message gets through to her. I catch the twinkle in her eye as if tears are going to flow but she pushes them back, trying to accept what I said as truth. I myself, know how hard it is to believe the good someone else sees in you, when you can no longer see it. Wanting her in my arms, I release her chin and pull her into my embrace and she comes willingly. Tucking her head into my chest, I hold her there as we breathe each other in, releasing her once we have both had our fill.

We pull apart as I hear Scott yell from upstairs, "Tate, could you help us up here?" I turn away from her and bound up the stairs to help the guys finish with the room. Walking into her room, I'm blasted with her scent again. I inhale deeply. It may sound weird but her scent relaxes me. It makes me content, like I'm coming home, whenever I enter her room. I've never experienced this before. Especially not with someone's scent.

As we are putting the final touches on the room, Tanya comes in, informing us she's leaving.

"I won't be back too late, I don't think," she says, as we follow her downstairs to the front door. "Don't forget to order some dinner." She leans into Tamsyn giving her a kiss goodbye on her cheek, leaving us in the lounge as she departs for the night.

"What do you guys wanna eat?" Tamsyn asks us.

"Chinese?" Rafe suggests, and we all agree as no one else has any other ideas to offer. Rafe must eat a lot of Chinese food as he has the takeaway on speed dial. We yell out our orders to him and he manages to order it all, without taking a breath. Rafe and JP leave to pick it up. It's the local takeaway store and is situated in the small group of shops, a few streets away from Tamsyn's place.

Tamsyn reaches up on her tippy toes, opening a cupboard above her head. I'm stuck in a trance, watching as her singlet rides up and I'm granted with a peek of the dimples on her lower back. My brain short circuits and my body takes over, moving me straight towards her. My hands are in control, they have to touch those dimples. I hear her intake of breath as I press up behind her and grasp her hips, touching her skin that showed itself to me. Holding on to her hip, I let go with one hand to grab the glasses for her she was struggling to reach. Pinning her against the cupboard, she can't move while I slowly lower one glass and then get another down. Once I've got five glasses sitting on the bench, I let go of her and step back, her touch lingering on me. She slowly turns around and rests her hands on the bench behind her, smiling at me.

"Thanks for your help," she says, which has me smiling in return.

"Ahem," we turn our heads to Scott who is standing to the side, fake coughing at us. "Ummm I think you two forgot I'm still here," he says, holding his laughter in. We all laugh together at the awkward situation because he's right, I did forget he was there. Whenever I'm around Tamsyn, I end up with tunnel vision and she is all I can see, while the rest of the world fades into the background.

It isn't long until JP and Rafe return, carrying enough food to feed a small army. As they unload the food onto the kitchen bench, Tamsyn grabs some plates and we all start piling food onto them. Picking and choosing what we want. There's wontons, dumplings, chow mein, fried rice, honey chicken and Mongolian beef. All the guys are busy loading their plates up when I notice Tamsyn's plate. All she has on hers is a few lonely looking wontons and some fried rice.

"Here, pass me your plate, Sweetness," I say to her, with my hand outstretched. She reluctantly hands it to me with a sigh, knowing I will add more food. She needs to start eating more as she is wasting away, before my eyes. "Do you care what I put on here?" I ask and she shakes her head. I go ahead and add a couple of dumplings, some chow mein and some honey chicken. Not too much food but more than the inadequate amount she had.

"Thanks Tate," she says, as I hand her now fuller plate back to her. We all move to the seats at the kitchen table, and start digging in. Tamsyn passes the glasses out after she fills each with some lemonade.

Everybody is too busy eating to talk, all you can hear is our munching and chewing in the quiet kitchen. I direct my gaze to Tamsyn quickly, to make sure she's eating. She's finished off her fried rice and is starting on the dumplings. Satisfied, I dig back into my own food and find the guys are gobbling theirs up, like they are in a race to see who can finish first. It doesn't take us long to finish off our plates. Scott collects all our empty dishes, except Tamsyn's as she's still eating, and he takes them to the sink and rinses them. He then loads them into the dishwasher.

"So what do you guys wanna do now?" Scott asks.

"I'm keen to chill with some movies," JP says, and Rafe agrees. I'm not fussed with what we do. Being close to Tamsyn will be enough for me.

Once Tamsyn finishes her food and rinses her plate, putting it in the dishwasher alongside our plates, we all head upstairs to her room. The boys fight to get their coveted spots and settle in for some movie watching.

"I'm choosing the movie," Rafe yells, as he snatches the remote off JP and flicks through, until he finds the one he wants to watch.

"You can't be serious?" Scott says, from where he's snuggled under his blankets on his mattress.

"What?" Rafe asks, bewildered.

"It's a romance. I didn't take you for the romance type of guy."

"He's a closet romantic," JP chimes in, laughing as he mocks his best friend.

"Shut up, I like Kiera Knightley. She's smokin," Rafe says, as he pushes play on Love Actually. Tamsyn pulls the covers back and hops in, scooting to the far side. She leaves the blankets folded open for me to lie next to her. I hop in and as soon as I cover us, she moves straight to my arms to cuddle; right where she belongs.

She drifts off to sleep instantly. I wish I could sleep soundly like her. My thoughts always keep me awake. They bang around in my head like bumper cars, making my head throb and it's impossible to sleep for any length of time. The boys' laughter has me telling them to keep quiet so as not to wake Tamsyn. She must be exhausted to have fallen asleep so early. It's not eight o'clock. I can't focus on the movie, not when I have this wounded angel in my arms. I still want to help her, to fix her but I don't know how, when I can't fix myself. How long am I going to keep pretending I'm okay? I can't keep living on the small amount of sleep I get each night. I'm not living, I'm barely surviving. I have cut my running down because I don't expect to find the broken girl by the dock anymore. It was a strong motivator to get me running at night. I've given in to lying in bed for hours on end, until my eyes get too heavy to keep them open anymore.

"Do you want to pick the next movie?" I hear Rafe say my way.

"Nah, you guys pick another one," I tell them, realising I missed the whole movie. I didn't get to make fun of Hugh Grant, doing his silly dance thanks to being zoned out and stuck in my head. Tamsyn stirs, probably waking from the sound of my voice.

"Is the movie over already?" she says sleepily.

"You slept through the whole thing," I inform her. That has her sitting up, wiping her eyes, then stretching her arms over her head as she yawns.

"I'll stay up for the next one," she tells me, as she piles the pillows behind her trying to get comfortable in a sitting position. I do the same and put my arm around her shoulders, bringing her into my side. She rests her head on my chest and slides her arm across my waist. "What are you putting on?" she yells down to the guys.

"Since romance puts you to sleep, how about we put on an action?" JP suggests. His ulterior motive is he loves action movies. I doubt anyone could sleep through all the loud gunshots and car crashes bound to happen on screen.

"How about Aliens? I love it," Tamsyn says.

"Yes! Sigourney Weaver is such a badass," JP says. "I'll run and grab snacks too. Tate, you want to help me? he adds.

"Sure," I say, jumping out of my comfortable spot, to race down the stairs with him to the kitchen. We open cupboards until we come across the snack stash and grab enough, we are struggling to carry it upstairs. We unload on the guys makeshift beds and they plough in, grabbing what they want. "You want anything, Sweetness?" I ask, over my shoulder.

"Salt and Vinegar chips if there's any," she says, from under the covers. I spot a packet and throw it to her, as I grab a bag of chocolate fish to munch on. I walk back to the bed, jumping over the guys mattresses as I go. When I get to my side of the bed, I unzip my jeans and step out of them. I was already too uncomfortable lying in the bed with them. I don't think I would get any sleep at all if I had to wear them. I have boxers on, so it's not like I'm naked.

Rafe sees me taking my jeans off so he stands up and takes his shorts and t.shirt off and then the other two follow suit. All getting comfortable and settling in for the night. Before I'm about to get into the bed, I see Tamsyn biting her lip and looking me up and down. Something in my brain explodes and before I can stop myself, I grab my shirt and pull it over my head and chuck it onto my discarded jeans. Tamsyn's eyes widen and plant themselves on the T.V. I have a feeling she didn't want to get caught, ogling my naked torso. I climb back into bed and lean against the pillows but she doesn't come cuddle me like she was before. She's stiff straight against her pillows and avoiding my eyes. I reach my hand under the blanket and hook my fingers into the side of her sleep shorts, pulling her towards me. She lets out a small yelp which has me chuckling.

"Come here Sweetness, it's skin. Nothing to be scared of," I tell her, as I place my arm over her shoulders again. She finally stops resisting and places her head on my now naked chest and slowly moves her hand across my torso, exploring and getting braver with every moment. She draws little circles on my side and it's so relaxing, it's the last thing I remember before I fall asleep.

Chapter 18

Pain slices into my wrist and it has me waking up out of my dreamless sleep. Heat under my cheek distracts me and I am disoriented for a second, then I remember Tate. The pain in my wrist worsens and I realise Tate has a firm grip on it and is squeezing. I can feel his body thrashing beside me, like he's trying to break free from something.

"Quinn," he says, through clenched teeth. "Don't go." I can hear the hurt in his voice. He must be having a nightmare. When I catch a glimpse of his face in the dark, I see tears coming from his eyes and my heart breaks for him. I start pushing at his side.

"Tate! Wake up!" I whisper yell at him, not wanting to wake the others who are snoring away on the floor. His grip on my arm loosens enough, I can shake his fingers off but he's still asleep. Now he's whimpering. I have to wake him up but I don't know how. Hoping this will work, I climb on top of him and wrap my arms around his neck, pressing my head into the curve of his throat. "Come on Tate, Wake up," I plead with his sleepy figure. His body takes a few more moments but he calms himself, his breathing evening out. His arms wrap around my body, pressing me against him tighter.

"Sweetness?" he whispers, not understanding why I'm lying on top of him. I pull my head from his neck.

"You were having a nightmare, I didn't know how else to wake you up," I tell him

"Sorry. Did I scare you?" he asks, sounding shaken.

"I'm fine. Do you remember what you were dreaming about?" I ask, wondering what could have tormented him so badly.

He hesitates for a moment and I don't think he's going to answer, but then he sighs and says, "Will you come downstairs with me? I don't want to wake the guys."

I get out of bed, reaching my hand to him. He shuffles over the bed to get off and grips my hand, as we creep out of the room quietly. I take him to the lounge and we sit ourselves down on the couch. We sit side by side but then Tate bends down and lifts my legs up and over his lap, so I lean back and wait for him to talk.

"Did I say anything in my sleep?" he asks me, shyly. I have a feeling he knows he did. Has this happened before?

"You said 'Quinn'. Does that mean something to you?" I ask. He bends his head, his shoulders slouching forward. His whole demeanor changed with that one name. It broke him. Who is this Quinn?

"She's my sister. My twin, to be exact," I barely hear him whisper. My eyes widen in surprise because I didn't know he had a sister, let alone a twin. I don't say anything, wanting him to gather his thoughts and tell me what he needs to, in his own time.

He draws in a deep breath and says, "Do you sometimes wonder why I was so drawn to you? Why could I see your pain when no one else did?"

My breathing picks up and with a shaky voice I say, "I wondered but I didn't know why."

"It's because I see my sister in you. I see her pain in you. It's the emptiness in your eyes sometimes mirrors hers. Or the tears waiting to be shed but you hold back." He's talking so quietly, I can hardly hear him. It's as if he's scared to voice what he's kept inside for so long. I don't want to distract him so I sit still, waiting for him to continue and listen. "Unlike your pain which I'm trying to heal, I ignored hers. I didn't think she was serious when she said she was sad all the time. She stopped doing activities she once enjoyed and hanging out with her friends but I didn't think it was anything to worry about. I thought she was fighting and having drama with her friends. She tried to talk to me once and I told her to get over it, it couldn't be that bad." He's rambling now letting his mind drift back to memories of her. "She tried to talk to me about it another night, and again, I blew her off. I told her I was too busy and was going to see my friends, and I would talk to her later. Then I left for the night." He lets out a huff and trembles under my legs. I slide my legs off the couch, go sit next to him and hold his hand in mine.

"Whatever it is Tate, let it out. You've held it in for too long," I tell him because I can see whatever it is, is eating away at him. I can hear the guilt dripping off his words.

"My mum found her later on that night. She had taken a whole bunch of pills. She was rushed to hospital and they pumped her stomach but the damage to her brain was already done. She's been in a coma ever since." He breaks down and cries, letting the tears run freely down his face. I crawl onto his lap and wrap myself around him, holding on tight trying to soothe him.

"Shh, let it out," I tell him, as I hold his shaking body.

Through his tears he manages to say, "She's been in a coma for a few months now and if she does wake up, they think her brain will be too damaged to function at all." I continue to hold him tightly, not sure how else to comfort him. He's always appeared so strong to me but he's as broken as I am inside.

"If she's in a coma, then why are you here? Didn't you want to stay with her?" I ask him the question nagging at me, not understanding why he is here now.

"My parents sent me here because I wouldn't leave her hospital room. The first time I saw her in her hospital bed, I clutched my chest, it hurt so much. I couldn't breathe. I thought I was having a heart attack. It wasn't until I sat down with Dr. Lawson and he explained I had experienced a panic attack. He said my fear of losing Quinn was so intense, my body didn't know what to do. He gave me some techniques to try which usually help. From that day on, I slept on the chair beside her bed. This went on for weeks before my parents put their foot down. They said it wasn't healthy and some space from the situation would be good for me. Hence why they sent me to stay with my aunt and uncle and JP," he says, as he wipes a hand down his face, clearing away the recent tears.

"Is there any chance she will wake up from the coma and be alright?" I ask.

"There's always hope. I'm praying for a miracle," he says sadly. He raises his eyes to mine and I'm shocked by the pain I see laced in them. I never noticed it before but it's there. I've been so caught up in my own head and pain, I never recognised the signs. You can see on his face something is clearly plaguing him, and the panic attacks were another sign. How wrong could I be? Tate was right. His pain helped him see a kindred spirit in me and helped bring us together.

With his whole hand, he smooths the hair on my head and tucks it behind my ear, never breaking eye contact. He brings his full lips to my forehead, and holds them there in a gentle kiss. My eyes close of their own accord, relishing the feel of his lips on me.

He slowly pulls back and says, "Thanks for listening to me Sweetness. I guess I was drowning inside, as badly as you were."

"No need to thank me, it's what best friends are for. Anytime you want to talk about Quinn or about how you're feeling, I'm here," I say, as I lift my shoulder in a shrug like it's no big deal.

As he's staring at me, it's like he can see into my soul. I've never known anyone who could make me feel like this with a simple look. My arms are still wrapped around his neck but there's space between us, so we can look at each other. A shift in the air sends goosebumps along my skin and I remember he is sitting there, without his shirt on. His taut body calls out to me to be touched. Without breaking my stare, he brings a hand up to my face and tugs on my bottom lip, releasing it from my teeth. I didn't know I was nibbling on it. He holds my chin between his fingers and I try to swallow the butterflies down threatening to escape from my stomach. He leans in, my eyes close and he presses his warm mouth to the corner of mine, out of reach of where I want them. He pulls away to gauge my reaction. He must like what he sees because a small smile tugs at the corners of his mouth.

"You're perfect, exactly as you are, Sweetness. I wish you could see yourself, how I see you," he softly says, into the darkness surrounding us. He leans in and I know he's about to kiss my waiting lips but the intrusion of the door opening, has him lifting me up rapidly and dumping me next to him on the couch. I'm too stunned to comprehend what happened, when my mum walks in the door, snapping me out of it. She's trying to be quiet as she locks the door behind her. Turning around, she spots us on the couch and gives us a quizzical look.

"What are you two, doing down here?" she asks, as she eyes Tate up and down, probably thinking we were getting up to no good.

"We were talking Mum, that's all. How was your night?" I try to distract her by getting her to talk about herself.

"It was good dear. I need to get out of the house more often, I think. I didn't realise how much I was shutting myself off from my friends with my grief," she says.

"I'm glad you had a good time. You deserve to have a break every now and then. Well we might head up to bed now, Mum," I tell her, as I pull Tate's hand to follow me towards the stairs.

"Leave the door open," Mum calls behind us. I glance at her over my shoulder and see the smile on her face. We get back to the room and Tate pushes the door so it is clearly open, not wanting to disobey my mum. I get back into bed and shuffle over to the far side and Tate gets in behind me. I face away from him, knowing he will pull me into his naked chest like he does. Wrapped in his warm embrace, he plants a kiss on the back of my head.

"Night, Sweetness," he whispers. And with a smile on my face, I drift off to sleep, disappointed we didn't get to finish what he was clearly going to start downstairs.

_______________________Tate_______________________

On Saturday afternoon, I'm lying on my bed, listening to music and remembering last night. My heart is lighter now after telling Tamsyn about Quinn. I didn't realise how much it was affecting me. All the pain I was keeping inside wasn't good. I don't think my parents made the right decision, sending me away. My heart is torn in two. On one hand, I want to be back by Quinn's side, in case the miracle I pray for, happens. On the other hand, I've found Tamsyn now and I don't think I could bare it, if I had to leave her. I need her as much as she needs me.

I can't believe it, I almost kissed her. If her mum hadn't walked in, I know I would have. It felt right at that moment. I hope it won't be awkward between us, she was fine this morning. I slept soundly with her encased in my arms and didn't want to get out of bed. Tanya had come in and told Tamsyn she wanted to take her out for a girls day. I gathered Tamsyn was excited about it, by the gigantic smile on her face.

JP and Rafe have gone to shoot some hoops but I couldn't be bothered. I don't have any energy today. More sleep would be handy but with my brain firing a hundred miles an hour, I don't think it's going to happen. I'm way too wired from thinking about my almost kiss with Tamsyn. How did I get so lucky to find a girl like her? I know we are both hurting. It's why I think we should wait to start something. However every time she is in my arms, it makes it harder not to make her mine. From the way she reacts to me, I'm positive she feels the same. I internally shake myself and try to move my thoughts away from this girl. She occupies so much of my mind these days, there's no room for anything else. My mind wanders to the dream; the catalyst for me, spilling my guts to Tamsyn.

It was of Quinn. She was lying in her bare hospital room like she had been the last time I'd seen her. I was standing over her for some reason, holding her hand, pleading with her to wake up. Her eyes had rapidly opened and locked onto me. It was like magic, she was awake, having heard my prayers.

She'd squeezed my hand so tight and said, "Tate, it's time to let go now. You have to let go."

I pleaded with her saying, "No Quinny, you can't leave me. You're my other half. I can't go on without you."

Tears were streaming down my face and she smiled at me and said, "It's fine Tater Tot, I have to go now. I love you." When I heard Quinn's nickname for me, my heart had broken in my dream. My unconsciousness could feel the ache it caused. She'd loosened the grip on my hand and I tried fighting her, clinging to her with all the strength I possessed but she started to fade like a spirit and then she was gone. My other half was gone, and I was left standing alone.

No wonder I had woken Tamsyn up. My pain must have leaked out of me, it was so strong. My brain is abuzz with too many thoughts now. Don't think. Don't think. Don't think. I switch my music up louder, hoping the bass will drown my thoughts out of my head, before they take root and overwhelm me. Music pounds into my ears, but the swirling images still penetrate through the shield I've erected, and reach their destination. The only way I know how to relieve the pressure is to run. I roughly shove my feet into my sneakers and I'm out the door in a rush. My feet pound the pavement as I sprint away, trying to leave the thoughts behind which haunt me.

Chapter 19

Today was a great day. I hadn't realised how much I miss hanging out with my mum. We used to have girls' days all the time. We would spend them however we fancied, whether it was getting our hair done, manicures or facials, massages or shopping. We've both been dominated with grief, we haven't made time for ourselves or for each other. Today we went and got our neglected cuticles taken care of, getting manicures and pedicures. I got clear polish on my fingers but they are a lot healthier than they were, before we stepped foot in the beauty salon. I wanted something bright on my toenails so I got a hot pink with a bit of shimmer in it. Before I can talk myself out of it, I snap a picture of my newly painted toes and send it to Tate.

Thinking of Tate has me daydreaming of our moment in the lounge. If my mum had walked in a few minutes later, he would have kissed me. I've waited so long to feel his lips on mine. I guess, I'll have to wait a bit longer, but at least I know he's on the same page as me. And what the hell? Too busy thinking about the near kiss, I forgot his breaking news. Tate has a twin sister. It's a pretty big secret to keep. I can see why he kept it to himself. Now I know what he's been holding in, if I playback moments I've had with him, I can see the pain behind his eyes in those moments now. It's like my brain blocked it from me before, but now the missing puzzle piece is in place, it makes sense and a light bulb has gone on. The light shines on all the times I've seen pain etched on his face but my brain didn't register what it was. Or else my brain knew I couldn't handle his pain, as well as my own, so it kept it from me. Losing my dad, I have some idea what Tate is going through now, although his situation is different. His whole family is stuck in a holding pattern, unable to go back and unable to move forward. Stuck in the now, waiting and hoping for something to change. I hope he gets the miracle he's after.

The guys cleaned up the mattresses before they left, but I told them to leave the T.V. in my room. Mum has a T.V. in her own room so I'm sure she won't mind me keeping this one, for a while. Now, I can watch movies whenever I want. So that's where I find myself after my shower. Tucked up in my bed, with a singlet and baggy pajama pants on, with

Aliens 2 playing. I might as well go through the whole series we started yesterday. I had managed to stay awake and watch the entire movie, while Tate was the one who fell asleep. I did get a tad distracted by his muscles under my arm, luckily I didn't do anything embarrassing like rub my face against his bare skin. That would have been awkward.

A knock at my door draws my attention to it.

"Is it alright if I go to a movie with my friend, dear? I'll be gone for a few hours. Will you be okay by yourself?" Mum asks me, anxiously. We had a good talk today and I told her I was past the low point I got to, when they found me in the shower. I told her nothing like that would happen again. I also told her although I loved having the guys stay over, I can't expect them to give up their lives to babysit me. I still want her to go out and have a life. She needs to, her life can't revolve solely around me. It wouldn't be much of a life, if all she is doing is worrying about me constantly. It wouldn't be healthy for either of us.

"I'll be fine, Mum. Remember what we talked about today? You are going to have to leave me home alone at some point, so might as well be tonight."

"If you're sure?"

"Yes Mum, I'm sure. I'm already tucked in here to watch movies until I fall asleep, so go."

She comes to my bed and leans down to give me a kiss on the head, softly saying, "Thank you, dear. I won't be long," as she exits my room. I hear the clicking of the front door behind her as she leaves. Breathe Tam. You can be alone for a few hours. You will be fine. I check my phone but Tate hasn't replied to my picture. He must be busy. I place the phone back on my bedside table and settle in, starting the movie.

I'm so engrossed in the movie, halfway through it, when my phone pings from beside my bed, I almost miss it. Distracted by the movie, my hand searches for it, not wanting to take my eyes off the screen, in case I miss a crucial moment. I locate it and open the text.

T: Hi Sweetness. Sorry for the late reply. Your toes are as sweet as you. What r u doing?

S: Watching Aliens 2. Mum went to the movies so I thought I'd carry on with what we started yesterday. How was your day?

T: It's been filled with thoughts of the kiss we almost had.

My heart rate speeds up and butterflies erupt in my stomach. He's going there. I don't know what to say. Oh my gosh, I better say something fast before he thinks he's scared me off.

T: Sweetness?

S: Yeah.

T: I'm at your front door. Want to come let me in?

The butterflies take off and start hitting the sides of my stomach, making me sick with nerves. I thought I would have more time to prepare myself before I saw him again. I throw the covers off and wipe my sweaty palms on my pant legs. Breathe. Just breathe. I brush my hair through with my fingers. Leaving my phone on my bed, I trek down the stairs and timidly open the door. There he stands, leaning on the door frame with one hand, waiting for me. The smile on his face is infectious and I can't help but return it.

"Hi," is all I can think to say.

"Hi," he says back. We stare at each other until he says, "Are you going to invite me in?"

"Oh yeah, sorry come in," I say, gesturing with my hand to enter. He steps inside while I close the door behind us.

Before I have time to turn around, I hear him whisper, "Sweetness," right behind me. I can feel the heat from his body so he must be close. He strokes a finger along my hairline, down my cheek and then moves my hair away from my neck, pushing it gently behind me. I feel his warm breath against my neck as he kisses me there. "You're so beautiful," he whispers before the warmth leaves me. His grip on my wrist spins me around and before I can react, his hands grip me under my thighs and he lifts me into the air, making my breath hitch as my arms automatically go around his neck to hold on. My legs wrap themselves around his torso as he pushes me gently against the door. His shirt is soaked through, like he ran all the way here. For a second, I see pain streak across his eyes then it's gone in the same instance, replaced by longing and need. Does he see the same reflection in my eyes?

"I'm tired of fighting it, I can't resist you any longer," he gently says, and he must see the want shining in my eyes because with a peek at my lips, he suddenly moves forward. I hold my breath, close my eyes and wait an eternity for his lips to meet mine. His warm, full mouth presses so softly against mine, I hardly feel the whisper of his kiss. He pulls away but my body takes over from my brain and my own lips reach out for his, needing to feel more. Taking his top lip in between mine, I kiss him and hope he will react. He rewards me by sliding his tongue gently along my bottom lip. I let out the breath I'd been holding and I feel him smile against me. He takes his time, tenderly pressing his lips against me. He pushes me firmly into the door and lets go of one leg, bringing his hand up to caress my jaw. His tongue gently mixes with mine and I get lost in him. His earthy scent surrounds me, increasing my need for him. I tighten my grip around his neck as we explore each other. It's over too soon and then we are pulling apart. He plants a small kiss on my lips before he puts space between us. His touch lingers after we separate. My breathing is so fast, I'm struggling to catch it. I can hear his own rapid breaths in the quiet.

He swipes his thumb across my cheek, back and forth, and I hear the smile in his voice when he says, "You can open your eyes, Sweetness." I slowly peel my eyes open and he's staring at me with a smile upon his lips. "Hi," he says.

"Hi," I shyly reply.

"It was well worth the wait," he says, holding eye contact. The butterflies are flying circles in my belly and I couldn't agree with him more. He leans in, pressing his lips to my forehead which is now my second favourite place to be kissed by Tate.

"Should we continue on with the aliens movie marathon?" he asks me. I'm still shocked by what happened, I can't speak so I nod instead. He steps back from the door but holds me tightly to him and carries me up the stairs. When we enter my room, he releases me and I lower myself to the floor, stepping back.

"Why are you so sweaty?" I ask him. He'd forgotten he was dripping with sweat.

"I was running and my feet led me here. They know where they belong," he states. He's staring at me and I see the pain creep in behind his eyes. This time it doesn't disappear. I can feel the vulnerability coming off him as he breaks eye contact and says, "Could I stay with you tonight, Sweetness? I sleep better with you in my arms." With his confession, my heart melts into a puddle on the ground.

"Of course. How about you hop in the shower and I'll find you something of my dad's to wear so you can take these drenched clothes off," I suggest, and he nods as he heads to the bathroom to get cleaned up.

I follow him and get a clean towel out of the linen closet for him. Our fingers brush against each other as I hand it to him and electricity pulses between us. I rush to my mum's room to find some of my dad's clothes for him. I look in his drawers she hasn't gone through yet. I find a pair of boxers that should fit Tate and in case he wants one, I grab a t-shirt. I bring the shirt to my nose, inhaling and getting a faded whiff of my dad. Memories circle for a second, before I push them aside. Just breathe Tam, breathe. I focus my attention back to Tate and hope he chooses to forego the t-shirt. I enjoyed him sleeping without one last night. Carrying the clothes, I take them into my room and place them on the bed and wait for him. It doesn't take him long before he enters and my eyes bulge out of my head. He has the fluffy white towel wrapped low around his waist. His hair glistening as the water drips onto his bare chest.

"I'll let you get changed," I stammer in my awkwardness, as I leave him alone in the room, closing the door behind me. I wait in the hallway until he opens the door.

"Where should I put my towel?" he asks, as I ogle him. My prayers are answered, he put the boxers on but not the shirt. I hold out my hand and take the towel for him, go back in the bathroom and put it in the washing basket.

I want to break the awkwardness so I bound out of the bathroom and cheerily say, "Come on, let's go watch the rest of the Aliens movie." I grab his hand and drag him along behind me to the bed. I can't help the smile stretching across my face, when I notice him push the door wide open, how my mum likes it.

Flipping the covers, I jump in, he follows and I curl up into his chest, relaxing in my position. We settle in, as I press play and watch the movie. Tate gives me a kiss to the temple and I let out a sigh, content for this moment in time to be here with him, and be safe in his arms. A few minutes pass and I hear gentle snores coming from him. He's fast asleep. He's untroubled in this state so I let him be, hoping he will find a moment of peace, from whatever thoughts plague him. Continuing on with my movie alone, I let myself relax into his arms which are currently wrapped around me.

Chapter 20

______________________ Tamsyn ______________________

I didn't hear my mum come home from her movie on Saturday night, but she gave me a small knowing smile as I said goodbye to Tate the next morning. She didn't mention anything about him staying the night either. I think she still has anxiety in regards to leaving me alone by myself and feels more comfortable if someone is with me. I spent most of Sunday daydreaming about the magical kiss I shared with Tate.

It's now Tuesday and I can't get it out of my mind. He hasn't tried to kiss me again, giving me pecks on the cheek or kisses to my forehead but nothing else. We haven't managed to have any time alone though so maybe that's the reason. One of the guys is always around. The air around us has shifted, more electric in a way. I catch his smiles when he thinks I don't know he's looking at me. Every time I catch him, he smiles wider, not caring he got caught, which makes me smile back at him. His smile is contagious.

As I'm wandering down the hallway to the cafeteria to meet the guys, I spot JP up ahead. He's pushing past people in a frenzy. What's that about?

"JP?" I call out, but he doesn't hear me as his path clears and he runs towards the cafeteria doors in a hurry. I quicken my pace to catch up to him. Pushing through the swinging doors, I see him crowded by more people, pushing to make his way past. My eyes shift to where JP is desperate to get to and I see Tate by the door lifting his phone to his ear.

<hr>

Tate

The vibration from my pocket has me distracted for a minute. Who could be calling me while I'm at school? I pull my phone from my pocket. It's my dad calling. I still don't want to talk to him, but I remember the day I didn't answer his call and what it did to Tamsyn. I lift it up towards me and swipe across to answer it. As I'm raising the phone to my ear, I catch sight of JP running towards me with utter devastation on his face. What's wrong with him? In a split second, I feel it in my gut. Unease settles in my stomach like a storm is coming my way ready to blow everything away and I'm stuck right in the middle of its path unable to move an inch.

"Hi Dad," I say, as I watch in slow motion as JP struggles to get to me. My dad talks to me but two words are all I hear. Those two words change my life. They shatter me. I thought I was living in darkness before but those two little words have thrown me into a vortex with no end in sight. I'm falling with nothing to catch me. My world has stopped. Everyone around me moves but I am still. I can't hear. My phone slips through my fingers drifting away from me. The tray of food crashing on the floor along with it. My survival mechanism is in overdrive. It's never had to perform this hard before and I think it has broken itself with the extra pressure to keep me safe.

JP is bent down in front of me but I can't hear him. Why is he bent down? When did I get on the ground? Wasn't I standing? People are rushing around me. Why are they rushing around me? Why can't I hear them? I feel as if I'm in an invisible bubble cut off from everyone else. It's quiet here. My bubble doesn't have much oxygen though. My throat is tight. I can't breathe. I'm going to suffocate. I scratch and claw at my throat hoping it will help rip it open so I can get some air into my lungs. I suck in short sharp breaths. I can't slow them down. I'm too far gone this time. As the world turns black, I see tortured blue eyes staring at me and my last thought is I want the blackness to swallow me and never release me. Those blue eyes can save me now.

I'm numb. People talk around me but I still can't focus on their voices. I'm scared if I let their voices in, I'll let the pain in along with it and that can't happen. It will destroy me. I peel my eyes open, I don't know when I closed them. I'm lying down now too. I don't know how that happened or how long I've been in this position. Why are the guys looking so sad? Are they talking to me? I can't comprehend what they're saying. I sit myself back up slowly. I am broken. My shattered pieces have splintered yet again and this time I think they're too damaged to put back together. Who am I kidding? They weren't put back together properly the first time. I duct taped them up. But over time, the tape has gotten loose and come undone. It's unwound piece by piece and left them dangling by a thread ready to fall at any time. Those two words ripped the tape to shreds and slashed the pieces right along with it.

Peaceful. It's what I think of my new found bubble. Haven't I been seeking peace this whole time? Embracing the numbness to keep myself safe. I think I've gone too far in that direction this time though. I don't think I can come back from this hollowness. Nor do I want to. I'm safe here. Safe in the quiet. Safe in the bubble. Safe being neutral with no feeling. Can I stay here forever? JP slaps my cheek gently. Why is he doing that? I'm not here JP. I've gone far, far away. You can't reach me no matter how hard you slap me so what's the point? I'm safe where I am. I will not come out. Nothing can drag me out. I can't remember what's sent me into hiding but it can't be good. If it was good, my body wouldn't have sent me away, would it?

My vision is becoming blurry. What is wrong with my eyes? Why can't I see clearly? Everything is hard to see now. Watery blue eyes are staring at me. Why are they looking at me? They're distressed. Tears are streaming down her face but I don't understand why. What's making her cry? I hope I can stay here forever. Not feeling anything. Not hearing. Not being.

Why is she cupping my face? I'm staring at her but I don't

understand. I can't hear what she's saying. Her lips are moving but I can't make out the words. The void has swallowed me like I wanted and I don't want it to release me. My mind has shut down, stopping the attack on my heart. It needed to protect my heart. It can't be good whatever it is. Sweetness. My best friend. My distraction. I forget what she was distracting me from.

She can't take it anymore. She climbs into my lap wrapping her legs around my waist and strangling my neck with her forearms. She's squeezing me too tight. I can't move though. Can't hold her. My brain and heart don't compute at the moment. I'm fried. I don't know what I'm supposed to do with her in my lap. My fingers twitch as if they remember something they want to do with her in this position but my brain won't tell my arms to move.

A familiar scent tickles my nose. What is it? It travels through my nose into my lungs. Oh no, it's broken me. I'm gasping for air again. I dig my nose into her neck breathing her scent in hoping to calm myself but it doesn't work. I cling to her small body hoping she can save me from this pain. My glass heart has hit the floor and a million shattered pieces surround me. There's no way I will ever put them back together now. What is the awful noise? My hearing is slowly coming back to me but I don't think I like this sound. It pains my heart to hear it. It's rattling my soul. Please someone turn the sound off.

"Sshh, Tate. I've got you," the soothing sound of Tamsyn's voice is a small reprieve from the gut wrenching sound. The cotton wool still blocks my ears so I can't find the source. It's getting closer though. My senses are coming back to me. Can someone shut up the noise, please. The pain of it is piercing through my soul.

Too late. My senses have returned enough for me to realise it's me causing the god awful noise. My gut wrenching cries surround me and as my brain turns back on, my heart gets pieced back together and then shatters all over again as I cry out in pain for my Quinny.

Chapter 21

My heart hurts for Tate. As I held him in my arms his heart wrenching sobs tore through me. It hurt to hear him in so much pain. It was as if he was dying himself. He couldn't calm himself down so I stayed on his lap holding him together the best I could. JP's parents arrived and they looked as wrecked as JP did. I didn't understand what was wrong with Tate until JP told me Quinn died. He never got his miracle. Never got to say goodbye. I know how that feels. It nags at you constantly. It's a moment you never had but you want so badly. A moment you keep chasing but you can never catch because the moment isn't possible anymore. It doesn't exist. So the pain in your heart expands, until it takes over and gets flooded with guilt. You should have known. You should have called them or been by their side. How could you know their final breath would be their last? I don't know. I don't think it's possible but the guilt is still there. Eating away at me because I should have been there in my dad's last moments. Knowing Tate, he will most likely be the same. He was already drowning in guilt over not paying attention to Quinn's pain before. I hate to think what is going through his mind now. Will he survive this?

He didn't register his aunt and uncle were there. I had looked over at Rafe and Scott and their faces contained so much worry for Tate. He was broken on the floor. He had collapsed from the shock. Luckily Rafe had caught him before he hit the ground, breaking his fall. With the help of his dad, JP had hoisted Tate up after I removed myself from his lap. As soon as I stepped away from him, his sobs quietened and the vacant look had returned to his face like he wasn't there anymore. He looked like a zombie. With his arms thrown over their shoulders, they'd led him away from the cafeteria, taking him home.

The bell signalling the end of school is ringing and I wander out to the car park. JP left with Tate so I don't have a ride home. I catch sight of Rafe and Scott coming towards me.

"Come on T, let's walk home," Scott sadly says, as he takes my hand. I like how he's trying to comfort me but his hand is wrong in mine. It's not the hand that belongs in my grip. I hold on tight though, needing someone to help me keep it together. We walk in silence through the streets, all of us absorbed in our own thoughts.

"Do you think we should go check on him?" Rafe asks, breaking the silence. I stare at his crestfallen face not knowing what to say. I desperately want to see Tate and cradle him in my arms but I'm also scared. Scared of seeing the blank expression on his face and not knowing how to help him.

"We should give him some space to be with his family," Scott suggests. I let my fear take control and agree with Scott so I don't have to face it.

The boys kindly walk me home. They said they would meet me at my house tomorrow morning a bit earlier so we could all walk to school together again. We don't expect JP and Tate to be there. I'm guessing Tate will fly home for the funeral. As I open the door to my house, I can't hold myself together and I fall to the floor. My mum hears my cries and comes racing towards me holding me in her arms and in between sobs I tell her what happened. I'm not sure how long we sit there on the floor in the entryway to my house but mum doesn't make me hurry. She lets me be until I'm ready to move.

"I might go take a shower Mum. Clean myself up a bit," I tell her, as I trudge towards the stairs.

"It's a good idea, love. I'll put dinner on while you do that, in case you get hungry," she says, as she turns to go into the kitchen. I drop my bag in my room and continue on to the bathroom. I yank my shirt over my head and unstrap my bra, dumping them both on the floor. I kick off my shoes and peel off my socks, then unzip my skirt and remove the safety pin letting it fall to the floor along with my underwear. I step into the shower turning it on, not caring the water is cold at first. I let the water wash away my tears with it as I crumble to the ground. Unable to hold myself up anymore and letting my grief take over. Grief for Tate's loss and grief for my dad. It all consumes me and I stay under the water until my tears have run dry.

I manage to pick myself up, wrap a towel around me and shuffle back to my room. Without putting on clothes, I climb into bed in my towel feeling exhaustion take over. I close my eyes, hoping I will drift off to sleep for a moment, needing a minute to breathe.

________________________________Tate________________________________

The numbness switch is easier to flick on now. I think I'll keep it on this time. It hurts too much when it shuts off. Tamsyn caused it to turn off. She makes me feel when I don't want to. I need to be numb now. Unfeeling. If I feel all this pain boiling inside, I don't think I will recover from it. How can I when my other half has gone from this world? Am I still a twin now my twin has gone? Do I still have a sibling if people ask or am I now an only child? How easily two became one. Now I'm half of a whole. If I let myself feel this, I will shatter. How can I put myself back together, when the other half of me has gone forever?

My dad was going to hop on a plane and come get me, but I convinced my uncle I could get on a flight tomorrow by myself. I'd be fine. So he conveyed my message to my dad. I'll be fine as long as I stay numb. I should never have left Quinn. I should have stayed by her side. I should have been there. The nightmare I had a few nights ago comes back to me. Was it Quinn's way of saying goodbye to me? Did she know she was going to die? Don't think. Don't think. Don't think. Thoughts cause you distress and this agony, you cannot handle.

Time escapes me. I don't know how long I've been lying on my bed, staring at the ceiling. I can hear JP and his parents talking outside my door, wondering if they should come in to check on me. They decide JP should come in alone, so he knocks softly on the door before he opens it, letting himself in. He sits on the end of my bed, not saying a word. It's a first for him. I don't think it will be long until the silence gets to him. He surprises me by lasting longer than I thought. He doesn't know what to say. I don't think there's anything I want to hear. Nothing can make it better.

"You okay, bro?" There he goes, I knew he couldn't handle the silence too much longer. I turn my gaze his way and he must see the answer written on my face because he drops his eyes to the ground.

"Have you heard from Tamsyn?" he asks, and the sound of her name has my heart picking up speed. I squeeze my eyes shut. I can't let her in. I won't. She weakens my survival mechanism. She makes it faulty. Blue eyes flash behind my tightly shut lids then they switch to green eyes. It's like they are one and the same. Two broken girls I couldn't fix. Don't think. Don't think. Don't think. I press my palms firmly to my eyes trying to erase the images. I can hear my once relaxed breath increasing again. Damn it. Not now. JP is shaking my arm trying to get my attention.

"Tate?" he yells at me, trying to draw me back to him. I try to quiet the thoughts working their way in. "Mum? Dad?" he calls, and his voice is already fading as my panic attack takes hold. He has his phone to his ear now but I can't hear what he's saying or to who. The numbness in my hands arrives and tingling shoots up my arms. It won't be long now. It doesn't matter who he's talking to as the darkness is creeping in on the edges of my vision, soon it will take me.

______________________ **Tamsyn** ______________________

My phone ringing draws me from my sleep. I stumble over to my bag by the door and fish it out before the caller hangs up. It could be Tate. I answer without looking at the caller ID.

"Tate?" I ask.

"Tamsyn, it's JP." I let out a breath at it not being who I thought.

"Is he okay?" I ask.

"No he's not. Could I come pick you up and bring you to him please?" he pleads, like he thinks I might deny him.

"Of course. I'll get changed," I tell him.

"I'll see you in a minute," he says, and I hear his car starting before he hangs up the phone. I rush to my dresser, grabbing the first clothes I lay my fingers on not caring at this point what I put on. My first thought is I need to get to Tate. After I've got clothes on, I run to my mum's room and explain to her where I'm going.

"Ring me if you need anything please," she tells me, as I hurry down the stairs and out the door. JP is pulling up near the footpath as I close the door behind me. I hop in the car and he pulls away, while I fiddle with my seat belt, trying to buckle it.

"What's wrong?" I ask, as he's in such a hurry and the expression on his face isn't good.

"He's been in his room since we got home from school. When I went in to talk to him, it sent him into another panic attack," he tells me. He pulls up to his house and we jump out. I've never been inside JP's house before so I'm nervous for a moment before my need to see Tate overrides every other emotion. He swings the door open and I follow his quick steps into a lounge area and down a hallway. He enters an open door and talks to his mum and dad who are standing there. They all move to the side and I catch a glimpse of Tate lying curled up on a bed with his eyes closed. He looks like he's sleeping.

"Tate," I say to myself, as my body takes over and leads me to his side. I crouch down in front of him and wipe his hair off his face. He stirs and slowly wakes.

"Sweetness?" he questions, as if he's unsure I'm here.

"I'm here. It's okay," I try to soothe him, but as I'm looking into his eyes, I see the exact moment something in him changes.

He pushes his palms into his eyes screaming, "No, no, no." His breathing is speeding up and I can tell he's on the verge of another panic attack.

"Tate," I call to him, as tears stream down my face, my heart breaking as I watch my sweet boy suffering.

"I can't, I can't. No. I won't," he's mumbling now, not making sense.

"What is it Tate? What's wrong?" he stabs me in the chest with his response.

"You. It's you. I can't do this. I can't be around you. You make me hurt too much, make me feel too much." He tucks himself into a ball and is rocking back and forth. I'm hurting him? I want to help him. How can I be making his pain worse? Then it dawns on me. He told me he saw Quinn's pain in me. It's what drew him to me. He saw Quinn in me and now she's gone and I'm a reminder of her. I'm drowning him without meaning to.

JP places his hand on my shoulder and asks quietly, "Maybe I should take you home Tamsyn?" Rivers of tears roll down my cheeks.

"Tate?" I beg. He stops his rocking and is still for a few moments. When he raises his head, I know he's cut himself off from me. He's gone again. His eyes blank. There's no hurt behind them, no life. He stares at me then slices my heart in two.

"I'm leaving tomorrow. I'm going home and I'm not coming back."

"What?" Both me and JP say in unison, both in shock at his admission he's leaving for good.

"I'm no good for you Tamsyn. You're better off without me. I'm no one's saviour." It's a sucker punch to the gut when I hear my name on his lips, and not the use of 'Sweetness'. I don't know how to help him.

"Tate, it's your grief talking. You don't mean that," I try to reason with him.

"Bro don't do this," JP tries to talk to him on my behalf, but I can tell it's no use. He sits there with his wall firmly in place, with his mind made up about me. There's nothing I can say to change his mind, I know this from my own experience with my grief. My heart cracks knowing I'm not strong enough to save us both. I've been where Tate's been. The void. The hollowness. I've barely managed to claw my way halfway to the top of my own darkness and still there's days where I plummet to the bottom, having to climb my way back up. I selfishly can't save us both but I can stop him from hurting more.

With tears streaming down my face, I break both our hearts by saying, "I can't shine enough for the both of us Tate. I see you need to be hollow right now to survive. I more than most understand but please don't let the shadows consume you. There's going to come a day when someone will offer you a lifeline, please take it. Let them save you like you saved me. Remember to shine, Tate."

As he hears my words, I think I see him wince but then it's gone like it wasn't there. I must have imagined it. Seeing what I want to see. I turn to walk out the door but turn back for one last glance at him. My sweet boy sits there, looking so broken, barely holding it together. It pains me to walk away but I'm not what he needs right now. If I'm a reminder of her, I don't want to be the cause of more suffering for him.

"Goodbye Tate," I softly whisper, as I twist around and race from the house. I sprint down the street, tears blinding my vision as I head home. Leaving my sweet broken boy behind, along with the biggest part of me belonging to him. The piece he's crushed on the floor into a million splattered pieces; my heart.

TO BE CONTINUED...

Playlist for 'Don't think. Just breathe.'

1. Catching feelings by Drax Project feat. Six60
2. Give me love by Ed Sheeran
3. You're my best friend by Queen
4. Air that I breathe by The Hollies
5. A groovy kind of love by Phil Collins
6. Before you go by Lewis Capaldi
7. Chasing cars by Snow Patrol
8. Who you are by Jessie J
9. Lost without you by Freya Ridings
10. You said you'd grow old with me by Michael Schultze
11. Gravity by Alex and Sierra
12. Dance with my father by Luther Vandross
13. Numb by Linkin Park
14. Unwell by Matchbox 20
15. Half a man by Dean Lewis
16. Is it just me? by Emily Burns
17. Sad forever by Lauv
18. Fall by Justin Bieber

Acknowledgements

Firstly, I'd like to thank my Dad, John Delany, my sister, Rachel Ayers and my Big Bubba Johno McGrath. Losing the three of you in the space of eleven months was so earth shattering for me, the only way I could deal with the pain was to put it down on paper. I've weaved parts of all of you throughout the book. This book is filled with a lot of sadness but also filled with an extraordinary amount of love. It's filled with the love I have for you three, it had nowhere to go except down on paper. I know the three of you would have been my biggest supporters. Without you, this book never would have come to be.

Secondly, I'd like to thank my little sister Rebecca Andrews. Who knew after all those irritating years of driving me crazy, you would come in handy in helping me to achieve this. Without you, this book wouldn't have turned out as great as I believe it has. For that, I am truly grateful. I'm glad I've had you to bounce ideas off of. If you weren't as enthusiastic about it as I was, I doubt I would have continued. Thank you for believing in me.

To my mother, thank you for being there on the end of the phone nearly every day, even when I rang to talk about the weather. I love you more than I can express and I hope you know how much. I will finish the trilogy so I don't leave you wondering what happens next.

To my five main men, TJ and my sons. Thank you babe for being supportive of me through this. I know you probably won't read this, as you aren't much of a reader. I want you to know, even though we drive each other crazy, I'd still choose you a million times over to share this life with. Kids, thanks for being quiet and letting mum write and for being so well behaved. Yeah right, who am I kidding. Don't stop being the noisy, boisterous, high energy little men you are. And always remember, you are never too old to give your mum kisses and hold her hand.

To Michael Pati Fuiava, my hunger buster brother. What can I say? You are amazing. The cover design is more than I could have imagined. You've given life to my characters in a way I never dreamt possible. Thank you so much for all the help you've given me in getting this book ready to go. I also appreciate all your help behind the scenes and marketing the book on social media. You're a great friend and I'm lucky to have you.

To my best friends, my sisters from different misters. You are the most beautiful souls I know and I'm honoured I get to call you my friends. Lena aka Booger, Debs, Keets, Chrys, Con, Rita, Roseanne, Bri aka Bumbum, Bec Ah You, Lisa and Jaime Addy. Thank you for sticking by me through all these years. I'm lucky my closest friends exceed a handful.

To my BFF Melz, God truly blessed me when he gave me you. No matter how far apart we are, you will always be my BFF. I love you with the fire of a thousand suns. Our green dress lives on in the pages of my book.

To my friends and family, thank you so much for being energetic and excited whenever I told one of you I had written a book. Your positive vibes kept me going. A special thanks to Wayne and Germayne for reading the book, giving me feedback and falling in love with the characters as much as I did.

And lastly to my readers, I hope you enjoyed this book as much as I did writing it. At thirty-four years of age, I didn't think I would be releasing my first novel. If you have a dream, chase it and don't let anyone stand in your way. You are wonderful and unique and there's only one of you in this world. So don't let anyone, or yourself, dim your light. Let yourself shine!!

Feedback

Did you enjoy this book? Would you like to give feedback? Did you know word of mouth is what makes the publishing world go round. If you enjoyed reading this book, please feel free to share your opinions or post a review online. We would love to hear from you. Or even better, let your facebook friends know and encourage them to read the book.

Check out my Facebook and Instagram or feel free to email me.

@ sarahdelanywrites@gmail.com

@sarahdelanywrites

facebook.com/sarahdelanywrites

About The Author

_____________________Sarah Delany_____________________

"Don't think. Just breathe" is Sarah Delany's debut novel. It is the first in what she hopes will be a trilogy. She is one of eight siblings, has a loving partner and is a stay at home mother to their four young boys. Writing this novel was a therapeutic way for Sarah to deal with the pain and grief she suffered in 2019 after losing her father but also her sister and one of her best friends. She's a New Zealander who currently resides in Brisbane, Australia.